THE SPIDER:
PRINCE OF THE RED LOOTERS

MASTER OF MEN!

PRINCE OF
THE RED LOOTERS

By Grant Stockbridge

ALTUS PRESS • 2019

CHAPTER 1
THE FLY'S PARLOR

RICHARD WENTWORTH swung down from the milk wagon and hustled a basket of clinking bottles toward the next brownstone front. His eyes looked sleepy beneath the straggling reddish hair that was part of his milkman's disguise, but those eyes studied keenly the darkness ahead.

He knew those shadows held police. For the Spider, they might well hold death!

Yet he must penetrate that hidden police line, must risk death in that apartment house halfway down the block or once more Loot and Murder would stomp their blood-clotted boots into the helpless face of the nation!

It had been a week now since that necromancer of crime who called himself the Fly had killed four men in an insurance office and walked coolly away with fifty thousand dollars; walked away and vanished even while police closed in upon him! And it had been a week since, his crime accomplished with suave ease, he had tauntingly challenged the Spider!

The front page of every newspaper in the country had blazed with it, had been plastered with four-, five-, six-column cuts of the personal from *The New York Times*, through which the Fly had spoken:

"Won't you come into my parlor?" said the Fly to the Spider.

1

THE SPIDER

Fifth Avenue was a shambles. A great hole gaped in front of the building the Fly had attacked.

Pardon the reversal, my dear Spider, and accept my apologies for the execrable rhythm, but believe that the invitation is nonetheless cordial. I shall, presently, reveal the address of my parlor so that only your keen mind will understand. I hope you will find it convenient to attend my little "at home."

THE FLY.

A week had passed, and the Spider had not been able to act. Because of that, his grip on the Underworld was weakening. The serpent of crime, long submissive beneath his iron heel, was beginning to rear its ugly head to threaten the people to whose defense Wentworth had dedicated his life.

He must, *must,* act at once. And to act, to learn the address of the Fly's parlor, he would have to pass through those police lines and seize the bait of the trap they had set for the Spider.

Wentworth was within two houses of the apartment now. He set down a bottle in a dark doorway and bustled toward the next brownstone front. As he trotted into the hot, small circle of a streetlight, sweat glistened on his bare shoulders. Plunging again into the shadows, he pulled up sharply and stared with simulated surprise at the entryway beneath the brownstone steps.

A MAN came out of the shadows slowly, a police detective with a straw hat on the back of his head. He walked up close. "You're not the regular milkman on this route," he stated.

Wentworth stared sleepily into the small, suspicious eyes of the detective. He jerked his reddish mop of hair in negative.

"Nein," he grumbled, with a thick German accent. "Das NRA all time trouble for me make. Das man iss off."

He flinched when the white beam of a flashlight flicked without warning into his face, then blinked sheepishly.

The man with the straw hat grunted, "Okay. Get going."

Still looking at him, Wentworth set a quart of milk and a half-pint of cream in the entryway, then trotted into the six-story apartment house. Was the detective suspicious? Were he and his companions closing in even now? No way of telling, but at least the Spider was inside the police lines, inside the trap!

The bait of the trap was a show girl who, out of a clear sky, had announced to the newspapers that she knew the Spider. She didn't, of course. It was obvious to the Spider that she was inspired by the Fly, that this was the revelation of his "parlor's" address that he had promised to make.

Ever since she had spoken, Wentworth had tried by every means at his command to talk to the woman alone. But police watched day and night, supplemented by special guards who took their orders only from the mayor. And the mayor had ordered the capture of the Spider!

When he had run himself to the top floor in an automatic elevator, he set down the basket and squatted beside it. His fingers moved nimbly, opening bottles. From one he drew out a tightly folded silken cape, from another a black wig. The basket had a false bottom, too....

Two minutes later, a hunchback draped in a long black cloak had taken the milkman's place. Lank hair straggled upon his neck. A dilapidated old man he seemed, but the eyes beneath the wide-brimmed hat were piercing gray and the smile upon the firm lips was gay. For Wentworth wore now a garb that even the policeman who had stopped him in the street would recognize. *He was the Spider!*

Silently he descended to the fifth floor and scanned the apartment numbers. Here police had lodged the bait of this latest of their many traps for him. A slight bitterness touched Wentworth's lips. The Spider was the greatest ally police had ever had in their ceaseless battle against crime, yet in their eyes he was a criminal, an outlaw, a man to be hunted down like a wild beast and slain.

Wentworth shrugged and moved on in his scrutiny of the doors. It might be bitter, but their hatred was understandable.

The Spider killed without mercy, mocked every constituted authority. The Spider did these things only to mete out swift justice to those who menaced mankind. He flouted authorities only because their lumbering machinery was incapable of coping with the brainy master criminals who scourged society. But these facts remained: that the Spider killed men; that in the eyes of the law he was a murderer.

And yet Wentworth hated crime. Paradoxically, it was for that very reason that he was legally, a criminal. Unselfishly he fought these monsters of the Underworld so that other men might lead the lawful, normal life that he himself longed for; so that others might enjoy the happiness of marriage and home and children that he must forever deny himself if he was to drive the menace of crime from the world. Because in his self-sacrificing crusades he must step sometimes outside the law, the law hunted him!

Despite police hostility, their continual traps and obstructions of his swift crusades, the Spider continued his work, slipping in and out of traps with smooth ease, helping them in spite of themselves.

No wonder the Spider was known as the Master of Men! No wonder criminals feared and police hated him! No wonder this trap had been set....

Soundless as night, Wentworth moved to a door labeled *5-C.* His right hand slipped to a compact tool kit strapped beneath his arm and a lockpick slid into the keyhole. In moments the bolt eased back. In this apartment was the bait. Here was the woman, Rosetta Dulain, whose redheaded beauty had been smeared over newspaper pages with the caption: *"The woman who knows the Spider."*

He crept now into the very maw of the police trap, drifted the length of the black hall and slipped to his right into the shadowed room at its end. Instantly the room was flooded with light.

Wentworth did not, as most men would, spring backward to the wall. He leaped forward, gun flying to his hand. His swift body, with its swirling cape, was a blur of speed…. Then he stopped and straightened slowly, eyes at once puzzled and amused. He confronted not the guns of police, but a man and a woman!

IT WAS the man who drew Wentworth's gaze first. He stood, slim and erect, against the opposite wall, upon his lips a smile that gaily matched Wentworth's own. He wore formal trousers—and tennis shoes. A silken undershirt alone clothed his upper body, and cradled in his left arm were two dueling sabres! As Wentworth regarded him warily, the blood began to pound high and thumpingly in his throat. He felt the throbbing of the thin half-concealed scar upon his right temple. He knew this man upon whom he gazed, though he had never seen him before. He knew this was the man who had challenged him so mockingly through the papers, who had braved the Spider's wrath. *This man was the Fly!*

The man bowed stiffly from the waist.

"Thank you, Spider, for coming so promptly," he said smoothly. "I thought I could count on you."

Nothing of Wentworth's tension showed on his face. Brows lifted enigmatically, he bowed without a word.

"As the challenged gentleman," the Fly went on, "you should have the choice of weapons. I hope you will not find the sabre too far from your preference in the matter."

Wentworth's glance flicked to the girl, the redheaded beauty of the newspapers. She stood tensely against the wall, a white hand clasping the neck of a negligee whose heavy silk, matching the flame of her locks, draped caressingly to her body. Her blue eyes were wide and frightened.

The amusement of Wentworth's eyes became slightly grim. Below were many police. If they were not already investigating, they would presently inquire into why a milkman had let his horse stand so long at the curb. But here was a graver menace than the police. Here was a man who likewise had readily pierced the police watch, who had gauged the Spider so accurately that he had actually timed his entrance into a trap! Here was a man who dared to snare the Spider, yet await him only with weapons for equal contest!

Wentworth stared at him, met the stony, black-eyed gaze, and knew suddenly that all his fears were justified, that here was a man who might terribly menace the humanity that Wentworth daily risked his life to defend!

Wentworth whipped off hat and cloak, tossed his automatic upon them. He no longer wore the milkman's sweat-stained singlet, but a shirt of fine linen. Slowly he rolled up his right sleeve. The slight mocking smile still tugged at his mouth corners and his gray eyes were debonair, but in his mind was grim purpose. This man must have behind him a mighty organization of crime! And the Spider—killed criminals!

Wentworth spoke casually. "Sabres will do nicely," he said, "but would it be impertinent, before we meet, to make sure of the identity of my opponent?"

Wentworth studied the man's alert face, and as he realized the intelligence and forcefulness of those level black eyes, the strength of that firm mouth and chin, his own disguised countenance set with his purpose. When men like this turned to crime, they constituted a menace that transcended plague and famine and wholesale murder! This man, turned criminal, might wreck a world!

The man smiled deprecatingly, as if he read the Spider's thoughts. He bowed slightly. "I have dubbed myself the Fly," he said clearly. "I welcome you into my parlor. I have only admiration for you, Spider, but your destruction is essential to my plans. Hence…" He proffered the sabre hilts across his bare forearm.

Wentworth smiled, caught a sabre and stepped back. How confident this man was of his ability! Yet the Spider's reputation as a swordsman had rung in the *salles d'armes* of a hundred capitals! The Spider whipped his sabre through the air. His eyes lighted. A sweet blade. He glanced about and saw all furniture had been thrust back against the walls. They would still be a little cramped… He faced his opponent.

"This is to the death, I assume?" the Spider asked politely.

"If you please," said the Fly. *"En garde!"*

CHAPTER 2
IN HIS OWN WEB

WENTWORTH FELL easily into position, knees bent, right foot forward, left hand on his hip. His right hand, grasping the sword, was raised to the height of his shoulder, point straight at his opponent's face. He felt strangely aware of those black eyes. There was a glint in them that meant death. Abruptly, Wentworth realized the reason for the man's confidence—the Fly's blade moved like a flash of light!

The Fly came swiftly to the attack, slashed for the left cheek, parried Wentworth's lightning *riposte*, lunged savagely. Steel clashed on steel. Soft-soled shoes stamped. The girl against the wall smothered a cry and the two men, sabres crossed above their heads, were breast to breast, smiling coldly into cold eyes.

They broke and Wentworth attacked viciously. His twirling sword was a flicker of light. But each cut, each thrust found only steel. The room rang with the singing harshness of the parries. Rosetta Dulain squeezed back against the wall, hands pressed flat and hard against it. She had forgotten that her negligee was unfastened....

The Fly's blade flicked past Wentworth's guard; its keen edge kissed his shoulder before a sharp beat of the sabre knocked it clear. Blood spread a slow stain over the Spider's spotless shirt—and the Spider laughed.

"Well done, Fly!" he cried. He joyed in the battle, in the swift, deft play of the blades, but within him a slow cold dread spread like death through his vitals. He realized that in this man the Spider's incredible skill had met a match!

Yet his fear was not for himself alone. If the Spider could not turn aside this menace, what chance did police have to stop him? The Fly, by removing the Spider, would have mankind at his mercy!

The glint of light on those flashing sword tips was mirrored in the cold anger of Wentworth's eyes. He leaped to the attack. He cut savagely, a heavy beat upon his opponent's blade. He sprang forward, in too close for a *riposte*, slashing again so swiftly that the stroke was almost a continuation of the previous blow. It was half cut, half thrust with the edge, viciously directed at the left side of the throat.

The Fly's parry was frantic, barely in time. Blood oozed from an inch-long gash on his neck. He sprang back, struck the wall and leaped aside from the swift following of Wentworth's blade. For seconds his life hung in the balance, then once more the two fought on equal terms.

Both had drawn blood, and now death was stepping closer. Its chill breath fanned the heated, panting bodies of the two who fought, yet both men smiled. There was determination to kill in the eyes, but there was admiration, too. These were men who loved the sword.

The Fly pressed his attack. He made a series of swift feints that were parried without the blades even touching. Then he sprang in, feinting again for the check. As Wentworth's blade came over for the parry, the Fly slipped his sabre under and lunged, apparently for the throat. Like light was the Spider's second parry, but swifter than light was the circling of his opponent's sword. It whipped about in a half *moulinet* and raked at Wentworth's chest.

If that keen edge touched, it would slash Wentworth from left shoulder to right breast. His blade was totally out of line. No chance there. No chance but to leap backward. No ordinary man could have achieved that spring in time to escape. Only muscles and mind trained to the split-second alertness and that superb coordination that had been the Spider's salvation in a thousand perils could win.

As it was, leaping backward, Wentworth slammed against the wall and felt the razor-cold touch of the tip. It just brushed the flesh beneath his right nipple, slitting his shirt, bringing a line of crimson. Then Wentworth was battling for his life: slash, thrust, parry, *riposte.* No mere feints, these deathly, lightning-fast strokes. The eye could not follow them.

Then, above the ringing slither of the sabres, Wentworth heard another more menacing sound, heard the shrill of police whistles in the street. In moments the blue-coated forces would pour in upon them. Death then to the Spider; slow, but no less sure than if that sword point that flickered now before his eyes slid past his guard and sheathed itself in his throat. Death, and the escape of this man whose half-admissions branded him a new scourge of Humanity!

Savagely, Wentworth fought. Inch by inch he drove back the Fly until once more he fenced freely and without the pressure of the wall at his back. Slash! Thrust! Parry!

Zin-n-n-g! The blade clashed. The Fly reeled back, empty

hands flung wide. His sabre crashed against the wall, rang on the floor.

FOR A half second the man stood rigid, eyes darting from his distant blade to the man who had disarmed him. Slowly the Fly drew himself erect, hands dropping to his sides. His chest panted, but his teeth were clenched. The mocking smile still quivered at his mouth corners. His eyes met Wentworth's without flinching.

Wentworth's heaving chest was red from the slow ooze of his wounds. He, too, straightened. He dropped the point of his sword until it rested on the floor.

"Get your sabre," he clipped. "Be quick, or our little *assault* will be interrupted. The police are coming."

For full thirty seconds the Fly met his eyes, then he bowed jerkily. "You make me regret…" he said. He straightened sharply and a pistol glinted in his hand, leveled at Wentworth.

The Spider's curse was as harsh as meeting sabres. He half started forward, but that leveled gun, the unwinking, stony regard of the Fly's black eyes stopped him. The distance was too great. Before he could raise the sword and lunge, that pistol would have poured a half dozen bullets into his body. He flung down his blade, folded his arms, contempt on his face.

The face of the Fly was white. He raised the weapon and leveled it at Wentworth's breast. The Spider's brow was calm, though anger and hate sent his blood leaping through his veins. Was this, then, the end of all his triumphs, to meet death at the hands of a criminal? He saw the tightening of the Fly's trigger finger. The muscles across his chest quivered with tension. He half leaned forward to spring, but something in the man's face made him wait…. The Fly lowered the gun, his jaw locked. There was a beading of sweat upon his forehead. For a moment he stared from heavy-lidded eyes at his victim; then he raised the weapon again.

"What's the matter?" jeered Wentworth and hope thrilled through him. "Does even an unarmed Spider terrify you?"

For a heart-thudding moment he stared again into the muzzle of death and saw the revolver's hammer ease backward for the shot that would mean death; then the Fly once more lowered his gun. This time it was with decision.

"I can't do it, Spider," he said almost apologetically. "You had me at your mercy, my sword on the floor, and you spared me. I cannot kill you now. It wouldn't be—sporting."

Wentworth laughed at him. "A gentleman killer!"

The Fly stared at him curiously. "I'm a trifle new at killing," he said slowly. "You should be thankful. Miss Dulain"—he spoke to the girl without turning his head—"in that small case beneath the Spider's left arm, you'll find silk cord. Tie him with it."

Wentworth heard the woman's slippered feet creep toward him.

"I deserve all your contempt," the Fly told Wentworth. "Either I should not have pulled the gun or I should have used it. I promise you we shall renew this little affair with sabres when the police cannot interrupt."

While he spoke, the silken cord was biting into Wentworth's flesh as the woman threw her strength into the knots. He was to be left here helpless while police crashed into the building. The Fly might as well use that revolver now. For the disguise Wentworth wore branded him the Spider as clearly as if he cried it in their faces. It meant the end, meant this shrewd man who called himself tauntingly the Fly could push on unhampered with his criminal plans.... Futile to fight this cord biting now into his ankles. It was his own invention—his own "web" as the police called it. The cord was scarcely as large as a lead pencil, yet it tested to seven hundred pounds!

Wentworth threw back his head and laughed sharply. The Spider was caught in his own web!

The man eyed him curiously, crossed to test the knots that the woman had tied. He thrust the helpless Spider back on a davenport, then caught up a cloak and the sabres, shoved the woman ahead of him toward the door. There he turned.

"We shall meet again," he said. "I promise it."

"We shall," said Wentworth grimly. *"The Spider swears it!"* The man met his burning gaze a moment longer, then nodded slowly. The door opened and the noise of the police invasion below swelled into the room. The door closed....

CHAPTER 3
IN THE POLICE TRAP

E VEN BEFORE the door closed, Wentworth's mind had been working like lightning on a method to escape and track down this mocking menace. If he could reach that dummy milk basket in the hall, he could free himself. It would be a work of moments then to strip off the disguise of the Spider and assume that of the milkman. Then he would retie himself and dive headfirst against the wall—and when the police revived him…. Wentworth lunged to his feet. They were bound together, but he could jump toward the door. He moved jerkily forward….

When police revived him, they would find only a bewildered milkman who spoke broken English, would hear a story of an attack in the dark hall by a masked man who wore a cloak.

They would have no trouble identifying that masked, cloaked figure. If the policemen saw a shadow that seemed to wear a cape, they cried "Spider!"

One more jump now and he would reach the door. He halted, rigid against the hall wall. That doorknob was turning!

Moments from safety he was balked! Were the police already on this floor? Wentworth felt cold despair writhe through him. His teeth set and he felt a thin scar on his temple throb with the anger of defeat. The door flung wide….

It was a woman, a woman in red. Rosetta Dulain. In her fist she held a knife. She sprang toward Wentworth.

The Spider twisted aside from the threat of that blade, but only for a moment. Then he stood motionless and let the woman come close. For she was gasping words: "The police! The Fly dodged them. I had a chance to—get left behind. He's got a hold over me, but if you'll get rid of him…."

While she spoke, she was slashing the silken cords from Wentworth's arms, stooping to cut them from his feet.

"Okay"—Wentworth bit out words while she worked—"I'll help you, but you must do exactly as I say."

"I will." The woman severed the last cord and straightened.

"Pick up the rope and drop it down the incinerator," Wentworth snapped. As she stooped to the floor, he sprang up the stairs and snatched his milk basket. Police were on the fourth floor now. He stripped off his bloodstained shirt and tossed that also to the woman. "Burn that, too."

The woman sped toward the kitchen. Wentworth squatted beside the basket. Black wig and the other makeup of the Spider vanished into its bottles. When Rosetta Dulain returned, the wound on his chest had been smeared with colodion; the milkman's dingy undershirt once more clothed his body; the reddish tousled wig and loutish face once more were his.

The woman came toward him slowly, hand once more clutching the silken negligee about her. Wentworth took off his shoes and straightened up with laughter in his eyes. Police fists were beating now on the door of the next apartment.

"Coome here, Rosechen," he said with a thick accent, "und bite mine shoulder."

He turned toward her the shoulder that the Fly's sabre had nicked….

The police beat heavily on the door of Rosetta Dulain's apartment. They hammered and grew angry and shouted. When the redheaded girl came to the door, dragging on her negligee over a sheer nightgown, she cried out:

"Wait a minute, cancha? What the hell is this, anyhow?"

"Open up," the gruff order came. "It's the police!"

17

She let out a choked scream, then fumbled the locks. The door slammed open, hurled her against the wall. A blue-uniformed man streaked past her, but the second cop paused to stare. She caught the red negligee about her, but not so rapidly that he failed to glimpse the sheerness of the nightgown.... He smirked at her, jerked his head down the hall, and she walked ahead of him.

The two crossed the place where Spider and Fly had dueled into the room beyond. A lamp shed rosy light upon a rumpled bed. The milkman stood beside it, head hanging sheepishly. He had one shoe on and he held the other one in his hand. The cop who had raced into the room was guffawing loudly.

AS THE woman and the other officer came into the room, the cop turned his head. "For Pete's sake, kid," he laughed. "Can't you do no better than a milkman?" He laughed again. "Hell, I'm going to see if I can't get on this beat."

He looked at the tooth marks on Wentworth's shoulder and fairly shook with mirth. He turned around and, weak with laughing, stumbled out.

In the other room, a man spoke with a crisp voice. "Well?" the voice asked coldly.

Wentworth stood still awkwardly beside the bed, holding his one shoe. He recognized that voice. It was the new special Deputy Commissioner of Police, Holland, who had been appointed by the city's reform mayor to catch the Spider.

Wentworth listened intently to the cop as with scarcely repressed laughter the man reported. "Found the milkman, sir. He had a heavy date."

Then Holland stood in the doorway, erect and stern-eyed. His glance flicked over the girl clutching her thin draperies about her, at the sheepish man with a shoe in his hand. Slowly the sternness faded. He raised a hand to his mouth. Another man peered in over his shoulder, a gray-headed man, sharp-nosed.

"Didn't the dame know we was watching?" this second man demanded. Wentworth identified him, too—Chief Inspector MacTivish.

Holland shook his head slowly, took off his dapper Panama. "So sorry we intruded, Miss Dulain," he said, mockery beneath his tones. "We didn't know you were entertaining." His amused glance swept Wentworth.

Rosetta Dulain began to curse, to complain shrilly. She shook her head so that her red hair swirled. She walked toward Holland, pouring invective upon him. Holland backed out with his hands raised defensively. The grinning men behind retreated too. When the police were gone and the woman had come back to her room, Wentworth donned the second shoe. There was admiration in Rosetta's eyes.

"Say, you're a slick one," she said.

Wentworth swept her a bow of exaggerated courtesy. "You're no slouch yourself, kid," he said, talking out of his mouth corner, Broadway-wise. He was abruptly serious. "Listen, the Fly gave you some orders. What were they?"

Rosetta nodded, eyes still on Wentworth's. "He said to go up to the Marlborough and register under my own name and he'd look me up."

"Then do that," Wentworth told her swiftly. "You can help me most by appearing to do as the Fly commands. Do you know his plans?"

The red head shook from side to side.

"What's his hold over you, Rosetta?" The girl's face clouded. She explained the Fly had learned she had a younger sister just finishing school. He had threatened to reveal to the girl what manner of woman Rosetta Dulain was. Rosetta raised her blue eyes to Wentworth's and they were glistening with tears.

"The kid thinks I'm the greatest thing in the world," she said slowly. "She don't know I'm Rosetta Dulain who does a dance bit now and then in the Jollities or rides a horse with nothing on except a few Indian feathers." She shrugged. "You know how it is… a kid like that…."

Wentworth nodded grimly. "All right, Rosetta. Play fair with me and I'll see the Fly is taken care of. I'll do better than that. I'll fix you and the kid sister for life."

The woman's eyes jerked wide on Wentworth. She came forward hesitantly, hands lifting. "You mean that, Spider?" she said hoarsely. "You ain't just stringing me along…."

Wentworth looked at her directly. "What the Spider promises," he said curtly, "the Spider fulfills."

He gave her brief instructions and left, carrying his clinking basket. He went out past the jeering police, religiously delivered all the milk in the block, and three blocks away in a *brauhaus* met the milkman he had bribed.

"Catch the girlfriend at anything?" The man grinned at him, getting up from a table and a stein of beer.

Wentworth spat disgustedly, sat down. *"Nein,"* he grumbled. "Dat *fraulein* too smart for me iss. Dese clothes, by der building superintendent get me, but iss nobody mit her." He turned his head heavily toward the bar. *"Zswei biere!"*

He sat staring straight before him. He had been successful in eluding the police trap after invading it and learning the explanation of Rosetta Dulain's boast. But so had the Fly! He had uncovered a menace that was the more threatening since he did not know the intent of the criminal.

He knew only that the Fly was keen-brained, that the man was bold beyond belief—had he not deliberately trapped and antagonized the Spider?—and that there was strength and will behind the man. He smiled down tightly into his beer stein.

The Spider knew that now he was fighting his equal in power and daring. And the enemy had won the first round!

CHAPTER 4
THE FLY CAN STING!

THE MAN swinging a cane down lower Broadway walked with a spring-heeled, happy stride. The noonday sunlight glistened on his silk hat. Gray striped trousers and cutaway were faultless. He tapped gleaming shoes up the wide steps of the Race National, swung right into the dignified lobby of the city's richest bank, and slanted toward a gray uniformed guard.

The guard bowed deferentially and the man looked beyond him to the mahogany desks placed at wide intervals on a half-

As he jammed in the last bundle of greenback, the cane swung again and the man collapsed.

floor some three feet above the level of the lobby. The rail along its edge was antique bronze.

"Ah, there's Sam now," said the man in the morning clothes. He slipped out a card. "Take that to Mr. Boughson," he said, and the guard, silent on deep carpets, strode toward Samuel Boughson, second vice president of Race National.

The man who waited glanced casually over the lobby. Two more guards in gray stood watching the several brief queues of depositors. They paid no attention to the man in morning clothes, but if Richard Wentworth had been there instead of striding briskly along Broad Street a half dozen blocks away, he would have been even more concerned over the plans of the Fly.

For the man in morning clothes was the Fly, and he planned in the next few moments to rob the Race National Bank of exactly one million dollars!

The quiet-footed guard returned. The Fly nodded absently and followed him to the elaborate desk of Samuel Boughson. He placed cane and silk topper casually on the desk and dropped into a chair the guard drew up before he left.

Samuel Boughson smiled noncommittally across the corner of his desk, ruddy full face bland beneath its neat crown of silver hair.

"What can I do for you, Mr. Hairstone?" he asked.

The Fly drew out a cigarette case of chased gold and, Boughson declining, lighted up. He dropped his hand carelessly upon his cane, whose ferrule pointed directly at the official's chest.

Then the ferrule of the cane folded upward with a click and revealed the muzzle of a gun. The bland smile stiffened.

"If you put your foot on that button," said the Fly pleasantly, "I shall have to press the trigger of this tricky little weapon. Now turn your chair sideways toward me. That's right."

He still leaned back casually, breathing out smoke with his words. The two appeared to be in careless conversation, but Sam Boughson, looking into the man's eyes, saw death. The ruddiness drained from his face. Stiffly he turned his chair about.

"That's fine," said the Fly. "Now then, Mr. Boughson, you and I are going for a little walk back of the cages. I am an official of the Bank of England and you are showing me around. Stand up. And I think you'd better smile!"

Mr. Boughson smiled. It did not matter that the smile was automatic and without warmth. Most bankers' smiles are like that. The two men got to their feet, and now it was the crown of the Fly's hat that covered the bank official.

"There's a gun in that, too," he explained, "and it's utterly soundless. When you were dead, I would pretend you had fainted and hurry for water. It would be a little while before they found you had been shot."

Smiling amiably at one another, the two men strolled past officials' desks; Mr. Boughson clicked open the electric lock of a door and they filed into the aisle back of the cages. As they walked, Mr. Boughson rattled off explanations. No one more than glanced at them, but twice the Fly stopped Boughson's details with a slow smile.

"My deah fellah!" he interrupted. "Really nothing so obvious as all that! Remember you are talking to a banker!"

Boughson's suspicious glance met the deadly calm of the Fly's eyes. He looked away hurriedly, and a twinkle came into the criminal's gaze. He was enjoying himself immensely. The scent of danger to him was like a trumpet call to a cavalry horse. It sent his blood coursing through his veins, made him tingle with life.

The Fly's gentlemanly appearance did not belie the reality. He was richly born and reared, but in the end, luxurious ease had bored him. Had his bent been altruistic, he might have become a second Wentworth, but something had been left out of his nature. His mode of life had encouraged selfishness, burned out the springs of kindness. He had come to think that the world was solely for his personal benefit and amusement.

So he had decided on crime for its unhealthy, perverting thrill. And he took no thought of those who might suffer for his "amusement," thought only of himself as his egocentric character dictated. He wanted to become ruler of the Underworld! It was a mad dream, selfishly conceived and fearful of conception. But this man had the ability, if he played his cards right, to fulfill that lunatic vision! Truly, the Spider had estimated the man correctly.

THE FIRST step in this dream of conquest, the Fly knew, must be the coordination of the city's criminal forces under his sole command. First he must establish a reputation. He had intended to accomplish that by killing the Spider. Balked in that, he purposed to rob the Race National Bank, single-hand-ed, of a million dollars....

He and his enforced guide had reached the vaults now. Within it two men were at work.

"Let us enter, my dear Boughson," said the Fly. They strolled in through the heavy triple doors, the outermost of thick steel with deals and massive bolts, the thinner plate with its simpler locks, the bronze grating inside that. Two men were at work within, one lifting packages of money from a small metal truck, the other checking items in a ledger.

The two glanced up as the grating opened, saw Boughson, and returned to their tasks. The Fly's cane whirled over, whacked against the skull of one man. He slumped to the floor of the vault. The other whirled with a smothered cry to gaze into the muzzle of an oddly shaped gun.

"Quickly," said the Fly. "If you wish to live, put the contents of that shelf in one of those bags and give it to me."

The shelf he indicated was laden with packets of large-de-nomination bills. The man glanced, white-faced, from Bough-son to the Fly.

"Perhaps a word from you..." the Fly suggested softly to the official.

Boughson's jowled face was like putty.

"Certainly, certainly," he said hurriedly. "Go ahead, Grimes. Do as he says. We cannot help ourselves; we must comply."

The man called Grimes swiftly shoved money into the bag, his back turned to the Fly. As he jammed in the last green-backed bundle the Fly had indicated, the cane swung again and the man collapsed.

"Now, Boughson," said the Fly softly, "pick up the bag and we will depart."

His breath was noisy between his teeth, his eyes gleaming pools of jet. Boughson took two slow, frightened steps backward before the menace of this suave man. He picked up the bag in a palsied hand and wavered toward the door. Just inside the grating, the Fly stopped him.

"Your smile, my dear Boughson," he reminded him gently. "It is not very convincing. If it does not improve, I shall have to dispense with your assistance." He lifted the gun again.

Boughson's lips were trembling. "Listen, Hairstone, or whatever your name is: You can't get away with this. As soon as anyone sees us leave this vault with the sack of money, they'll turn in an alarm. You are trapped. Give up this crazy plan."

The Fly's mouth opened and his breath came out, but if it was laughter, it was silent. "You forget my pistol makes no sound," he said. "Go on out. And—don't forget to smile!"

Boughson walked out of the vault and a gray-clad guard turned slowly. At sight of the sack of money, his face stiffened. His eyes jerked toward Boughson. The crown of the Fly's silk hat turned on the man and there was a subdued metallic clunk from within it. The guard's face continued stiff, but now it was surprised instead of puzzled.

The Fly looked swiftly about. Three other men and a girl were visible. Only the girl was looking toward them. Her mouth opened, and the Fly's hidden pistol spoke again. She fell while the guard still swayed on his feet, and the Fly's pistol spoke three times more while the man collapsed slowly, joint by joint.

The Fly jostled Boughson swiftly down the line of cages. They had passed through the door into the outer offices when the burglar alarm outside the bank clanged into heart thudding bedlam. Immediately the three guards in the lobby drew revolvers and peered about tensely.

Boughson, at the Fly's orders, stopped and stared back the way he had come. The floor where they stood was higher than the lobby. The bag was below the level of desks. The three guards moved up to the line of cages.

FRIGHTENED WOMEN screamed; men shouted. Several customers darted for the doors, but their exit was blocked by a fourth guard who patrolled the hall outside. He shouted at the crowd. The Fly turned toward Boughson. "I think you'd better try to quiet those customers at the door," he said. "And you can let me out at the same time. Here, boy!"

He called one of a half dozen office boys standing in an excited group and signed him to take the bag from Boughson. The boy sprang alertly forward and followed as Boughson hurried across the lobby with the quick striding Fly at his heels. The guard at the door spun toward them, stared over the heads of the customers bunched against the glass panels in panic.

The gun's metallic note sounded dully again and the guard fell. The Fly knocked the office boy out with his cane and seized the bag. A guard cried out toward the rear of the bank. Guns banged there, but the bullets flew high. The guards feared to fire into the crowd.

The shots completed the demoralization of the customers. They charged the glass doors, no longer blocked by a uniformed man. As they slammed into the hall of the office building, the Fly went out with them, thrusting Boughson ahead. A door panel smashed and tinkled to the floor.

The crowd poured to the left toward the street. The Fly jerked Boughson's arm and hustled him to the right toward the bank of ten elevators that served the offices above. They entered the fifth one together.

"Quickly! Go up!" the Fly ordered. "We just got the loot away from the robbers and... Up, son! Up!"

The operator threw them one swift glance, saw Boughson's frightened heavy face and the elevator shot upward. The Fly relieved Boughson of the bag of money. The man stared into his face fixedly and suddenly his eyes widened.

"You!" Boughson cried. "I know you now! You're...."

Pain distorted his jowled face. He gasped, doubled slowly forward. The Fly whirled from him, struck down the elevator boy with his cane and took the control of the car. On the twentieth floor he stopped it, got out, and allowed the sliding door to clang shut.

His gun was ready, but no one was in sight. He went down the hall three doors, crossed to a window, and threw out hat, cane, and, swiftly then, all his outer clothing. There was a stack of manila envelopes on the desk.... Seven minutes later a man dressed in a quiet business suit strolled out of his office and dropped a large number of manila envelopes down the mail chute in the hall.

He ran a manicured hand smoothly over his hair and smiled at the mail chute. He had, singlehanded, robbed a rich bank of a million dollars. He had performed a coup which would at once win for him a place in crookdom's hall of fame. Of course, he had had to kill seven or eight persons, one of them a very comely girl…. He nodded to the chute and strolled down the hall.

CHAPTER 5
THE FLY'S SIGNATURE

WENTWORTH HAD just turned from Wall Street into Broadway when the alarm of the Race National Bank hurled its clamor into the crowded noonday street. He was in action before that lunch-hour rush had more than begun to recognize the sound.

He darted to the middle of the street and, dodging taxis and a lumbering streetcar, sprinted toward the bank. The August sun bombarded the pavement with white heat; and girls in summery white and coatless men in straw hats stared wide-mouthed after him.

Someone cried "Thief!" and several began a half-hearted pursuit, but it was too hot. They quit within a block. Wentworth overtook a gray-shirted traffic cop slapping big feet toward the bank.

"Grab a taxi!" Wentworth yelled as he went past. "Get ready to chase the bandits!" A half minute later he leaped for the steps of the bank. A gush of fleeing men and women buffeted him.

"Holdup!" a man yelled hoarsely. "Holdup!"

Wentworth wormed to the right of the stream of the stampede, fought his way along the wall and into the building. At the precise instant Wentworth entered, the Fly, in an elevator passing the eleventh floor, was murdering Samuel Boughson. He had left no one to betray him, nothing to indicate his line of retreat.

Wentworth dived for the glass doors of the bank itself, springing over the body of a guard, past an unconscious office boy. Another guard, charging toward him, flung up a pistol.

"I'm a policeman!" Wentworth shouted. "Where are the bandits?"

The guard held his shot, puffed up to Wentworth.

"Ain't seen one," he panted out, "but them cages is full of dead men!"

Wentworth pivoted on his heel, sweeping the bank lobby with a single, all-seeing glance. No one save excited officials in the place, armed guards staring about them in bewilderment. Wentworth raced into the hallway. There was only one exit, the one by which he had entered, and he was sure the bandits had not escaped there. The elevators were just to his right. The uniformed starter was standing dazedly against the wall.

As Wentworth strode up to him, the Fly, twenty floors above, had stripped off all his clothing and thrown it out the window.

Wentworth spoke to the elevator starter curtly, but without excitement. If he further bewildered the man, it would take minutes to get information from him.

"Who left and took an elevator just after the alarm went off?" he asked.

The man stared at him with scared eyes, forehead wrinkled like a monkey's. "Who left the bank?" he repeated woodenly; then his body jerked. "Mr. Boughson," he stammered. "Mr. Boughson and another man in a silk hat. They had a bag…."

"Which car?"

The starter turned to the panel on the wall behind him, a panel in which series of light bulbs in vertical lines indicated the position of the ten elevators. Three cars were rising, bulbs flashing off and on in upward sequence indicated. Four were coming down and two were at the first floor. The tenth row of lights, the central one, was entirely dark except for a bulb near the top. That light burned without blinking. The car was stationary at the twentieth floor.

The starter's blue-coated arm stretched out rigidly, the finger trembling as it indicated that small round dot of yellow light.

"That's the one, sir," the man stammered. "That's the one. Number Five."

"Stop all cars," Wentworth ordered. "Don't let one move."

He whirled into an elevator. "Twenty," he snapped, "and don't stop until you get there. Police business."

The car, empty except for Wentworth and the boy, soared with silent speed. The operator overshot the twentieth floor and lost precious seconds juggling for the proper level.

When the door slid open, Wentworth bounced out shouting to the boy to follow to Car 5. The operator's key opened the stalled elevator's door and Wentworth flung inside. Boughson lay on his face and Wentworth turned him over hurriedly. The neat gray head hung back limply, and the floor was black with blood; from the banker's chest something round and golden protruded—the hilt of a knife.

Staring at that knife, Wentworth ground out a curse low in his throat. His eyes widened, then narrowed to ice-gray slits and he jerked to his feet. He knew now who had looted the bank. He knew who had filled the tellers' cages with dead men. For the hilt of that murderous knife was tipped with a golden fly!

WENTWORTH SPUN toward the prone operator of Elevator 5, then realized abruptly that the door was closed. He yanked it open, sprang to the hall and pulled up short, staring into a leveled gun. Behind it crouched Deputy Commissioner Holland.

"Quickly," Wentworth spat at him. "The bandit is on this floor."

Holland stiffened slowly from his crouch behind the gun. "How do you know?" he asked swiftly.

Wentworth jerked his head toward the elevator cage. "Boughson's in there with a knife through his heart. Elevator starter said Boughson came out with a man in a top hat and carrying a bag. Come on."

He whirled up the hall; then seeing the floor indicators above the elevator door, he halted and cursed. "The elevators are still running. I told that starter…."

He darted into an office, snatched a phone from the desk of a girl, rang the starter's desk. Before the gruff voice of a policeman answered, the girl had her hands on her hips and was bawling him out.

Wentworth ignored her, bit out orders to the policeman: "Don't let anybody out of the building. The bandit is a blond man with black eyes, just under six feet, weight one eighty. He wore a silk hat and morning clothes at the time of the robbery, but may have changed now. Hold anybody of that description no matter how he's dressed. Broadcast that description. Holland's orders."

As Wentworth talked, he turned to face Holland and found the Deputy Commissioner's blue eyes narrowed suspiciously. Wentworth lowered the phone from his mouth and asked: "Any further orders to give the sergeant?"

Holland said, "No, thanks." The words were quiet and expressionless. Wentworth hung up, nodded to the girl who still protested vehemently. The closing door cut off her shrilling voice.

"All right, all right," Wentworth said shortly to Holland. "I know you want to know how I got the description. I'll tell you later. Let's go downstairs."

Wentworth jabbed the elevator signal viciously. In his eagerness to trap the Fly he had given out information which the Spider had obtained—and which Wentworth had no reason to know. No one had survived the Fly's previous holdup to describe him. He must swiftly devise some explanation. Holland knew him socially, knew that he was an amateur criminologist. But Holland was privy also to the information of police, that Wentworth had been accused not once, but many times, of being the Spider. It was Holland's specific job to catch the Spider. He had been appointed by the reform mayor, W.O. Purviss, for precisely that purpose. If he could seize on this as an excuse to hold Wentworth….

"Well," said Holland at his shoulder, "how did you get that description?"

Wentworth sensed the hostility in his voice. He turned with a slow, frank smile.

"It's obvious," he said, "that I have better European correspondents than you do."

"Is that an explanation?" Holland was still quiet. His very lack of excitement was ominous. He was a blond man of Wentworth's own height, with eyes of frosty blue. His lean body was taut with readiness. Wentworth could have told him it was better to relax when you expected swift action….

"That's part of the explanation," Wentworth said, still smiling. "Boughson is dead in Cage No. 5 with a knife through his heart. The head of that knife is shaped like a fly. That means that the Fly the papers have been howling about is the same who operated in Europe a few years back. I phoned his description to the sergeant in the hall."

Holland frowned. "I'm positive there has been no such criminal known as the Fly in Europe," he said heavily.

Wentworth laughed. "I said I had better European correspondents than you." An elevator door slammed open and two uniformed police stepped out. Holland turned to them abruptly. "There are two dead men in Elevator 5," he said. He pointed toward the car, then cursed and flung himself toward the elevator that had discharged the police.

"Down fast!" he barked. "Elevator 5 is moving down, moving with two dead men in it!"

CHAPTER 6
ANOTHER SHREWD BLOW

THE ELEVATOR jerked into swift downward motion.
"Geez, Commissioner," one of the cops gulped. "Is a dead man running that elevator?"

Holland clipped out words, "Most likely it's the murderer. He could easily have slipped into that car while we were phoning downstairs."

The split seconds of descent dragged out into seeming minutes. Wentworth stood well back from the door, frowning thoughtfully. If that was the Fly, he would be insane to run a car of dead men to the main floor where police were thick....

"Three!" Wentworth ordered sharply.

The car was flashing past the fourth floor, and subconsciously, the boy threw the lever. Holland cursed and whirled. The door opened and Wentworth darted out. He cried out in triumph. The indicator above the door of Car 5 was stationary at three.

"The key, the key to the door!" he shouted.

Holland, at his shoulder, echoed the order excitedly. The elevator operator inserted a long peg-like key and the two police stepped forward with drawn guns. The door slid back. Two men

37

lay motionless on the floor, one in uniform, the other the dead banker. Wentworth raced for the steps, went down three at a time, and skated out on the polished floor of the lobby. A half dozen policemen spun with drawn guns and he studied each one of their faces shrewdly. None fitted the Fly's description.

"Who came down these steps ahead of me?" he demanded.

The cops blinked at him. A sergeant shook his head slowly. "No one, sir," he insisted.

Holland slammed out of an elevator. "Any luck, Wentworth?"

Wentworth shook his head, the puzzled frown more intense upon his forehead. Holland shouted orders to search the building minutely, every office, every closet, every storage room. Chief Inspector MacTivish stalked out of the bank offices.

"Seven dead in there," he reported. "Six men and a girl, all killed with a very small caliber gun. Doc says he thinks it was an air pistol. They're checking to see how much was taken, but it looks like over a million. We found a guard that took this guy to Boughson. The description you phoned down fitted him to a T." There was admiration in his voice. He lifted a hand slowly

Richard Wentworth

and scratched the tip of his sharp nose. "Don't see how you got it so fast."

Holland turned to face Wentworth. "Black eyes and all?" he asked the inspector.

"That's right," MacTivish nodded.

Holland kept his eyes on Wentworth. "If it weren't for that

one thing," he said slowly, "I'd say that the Fly was another name for the Spider."

Wentworth's mouth tightened into a thin smile. "Don't let that worry you," he said curtly. "If I were hard to put to it, I think I might manage to turn gray—or blue eyes—black." He spun on his heel.

"Just a minute, Wentworth," Holland called.

"I'll see you in Kirkpatrick's office," Wentworth clipped back over his shoulder. A policeman moved to intercept him, but Wentworth ignored the man, and when Holland did not call again, the officer stepped aside.

A taxi sped Wentworth to Center Street and he went rapidly to the office of his friend Stanley Kirkpatrick, Commissioner of Police.

Hand on the knob of the outer office door, Wentworth paused. A man's angry voice beat against the ground glass panel. It was the voice of W.O. Purviss, the reform mayor, and there was a shrill tension in it. Wentworth shoved quietly into the outer office. The mayor and Kirkpatrick stood before the door of the Commissioner's private office, two tall, angrily glaring men.

"I'll tell you once more," Kirkpatrick said in his precise, cold voice. "I have been out of the office all morning on that wild-goose chase you ordered. If you will step aside from the door, we'll go in and see if there has been such a tip."

Mayor Purviss' roached black hair was disordered with the violence of his head jerks. "There has been a tip!" he asserted belligerently. "You deliberately ignored the information, left the office...."

"At your orders, my dear Purviss," Kirkpatrick told him coolly. He saw Wentworth and waved a hand carelessly. "Mind waiting a moment, Dick?"

PURVISS THREW a quick angry stare at Wentworth, black eyes snapping, then pulled his left hand out from behind him and thrust a memorandum pad beneath Kirkpatrick's nose. "Explain that!" he shouted. "Just explain that!"

Wentworth could see Kirkpatrick's fury in the stiffness of his back. "Take that out of my face," Kirkpatrick ordered sharply. Mayor Purviss jerked his hand away, startled by the whip of Kirkpatrick's voice.

"So you have been prowling in my office?" Kirkpatrick demanded.

"When my appointees fail in their duty," Mayor Purviss said vehemently, jerking his black hair with his nods, "it is my duty to investigate." He raised the pad and slapped it with the back of a pudgy hand. "This pad bears a notation in your own handwriting to watch out for a holdup of the Race National this morning. It was robbed of a million dollars and eight or nine persons were killed."

Kirkpatrick stared blankly at the mayor for a full minute, then he took the memorandum pad. A quick frown wrinkled his forehead and slowly his fingers went to his pointed black mustache. Wentworth recognized that gesture. It meant his friend was worried.

Mayor Purviss was yapping at him like a small, spiteful dog. "I'll expect your resignation within the hour," he declared. "Send Jack Holland to me when he returns. He's doing your job for

41

you over at Race National." Purviss' bouncing stride took him quickly from the office.

Wentworth's mock-courteous bow was ignored and he crossed briskly to Kirkpatrick. "What's got into W.O. Purviss?" he asked.

Kirkpatrick held out the memorandum pad silently, eyes still worried. "It's a very clever forgery," he said slowly, "but there's no use arguing with Purviss. I'll resign."

"But, Kirk—"

Kirkpatrick shook his head. "That will be the best way. It's apparent somebody wants me out. Perhaps, Dick, you'll help me find out who it is?"

Wentworth said slowly, "I know who it is."

Kirkpatrick's startled stare was a question.

"It's the Fly," said Wentworth.

At Kirkpatrick's puzzled inquiry, Wentworth explained in detail about the Fly, but he told of the adventures of the Spider as if he had heard of them from some third person. It was his usual device with the Commissioner. His work as the Spider was an open secret between them. Wentworth never admitted the fact, but Kirkpatrick, lacking proof, was convinced of it.

"I approve of the activities of the Spider, Dick," he had said. "But that's unofficial. If I ever get evidence against you, I'll prosecute to the last ounce of my ability. I cannot neglect my duty. Meantime, if the police can help the Spider in any way...."

So Wentworth maintained the outward forms of secrecy as he told about the Fly. "It is apparent to me," Wentworth said slowly, "that this Fly is bent on some undertaking of enormous menace to the city. His coup today must be only a beginning, yet he got a million dollars and killed nine persons!

"I say it is only a beginning because it would not have been necessary to kill the Spider or remove you from office if this one feat were all he planned!"

The two men sat in Kirkpatrick's private office now and Wentworth rose and crossed to the window, peered out into the street. The hot sun beat against the stone wall here. On the other side, in deep shade, people moved listlessly. Men carried their coats and fanned themselves with straw hats.

"I never have felt so baffled," Wentworth said over his shoulder. "When a man has allies, it is easy to fight him. When he works alone and will not reveal his plans to anyone…."

Kirkpatrick crossed to his side, threw an arm about his shoulders. "We'll get him," he said shortly.

Wentworth laughed wryly, "If he doesn't get us first."

The door opened with a light warning knock and the two turned slowly to confront Jack Holland. He came straightforwardly to Wentworth, offered his hand. "I'm sorry if I seemed unduly suspicious," he said, and his smile was pleasant. "It was foolish of me and I need your help badly. To tell the truth, Purviss was responsible for the whole business."

WENTWORTH GRIPPED his hand hard. "Forget it," he said.

Holland shook his head emphatically. "I don't want to forget it," he said. "You know Purviss appointed me to catch the Spider. He pointed out that you had been accused many times of being the Spider and had wormed out of it by trickery. By trickery and..." He turned to Kirkpatrick.

"Purviss intimated that you were too friendly with the Spider to turn him in." Holland sighed, then grinned.

"There," he said, "I'm glad to have made a clean breast of it. I've decided that Purviss is using me to advance some political scheme and I'm going to resign."

Kirkpatrick clapped Holland on the shoulder. Holland was the younger man, but he had an upright manliness about him, a level eye and square-cut jaw that bespoke of a steadiness and intelligence beyond his years. Kirkpatrick's temples were beginning to gray and his eye corners bore crinkles of humor and shrewdness.

"Better wait until you see Purviss again," he said. "Purviss just demanded my resignation and then asked that you be sent to him."

Holland frowned. "I won't take the job," he said stubbornly. "I won't. I'll see Purviss and tell him he's making a big mistake. You know more about this business in five minutes than I would in five years."

Kirkpatrick picked up the memorandum pad and placed it in Holland's hands. The younger man read it, looked up startled. Kirkpatrick explained.

"But that's ridiculous of Purviss." Holland asserted. "I'll tell him so."

"It would be better if you accepted," Wentworth put in. "Kirk and I will be glad to help, and maybe we can clip this Fly's wings and learn just why Purviss is so anxious to get Kirk out."

Holland stared at him wildly. "You're not saying that Purviss and the Fly...."

Wentworth raised his brows. They were peaked and slightly mocking.

"I'm not saying anything," he said lightly. "What did you find out after I left?"

Holland put the memorandum pad on the desk and stood frowning at it. "MacTivish found another man who had seen the Fly," he said. "It was Joe Stull. He said he was just going out to an early lunch when the man passed him to see Bough-son...."

Wentworth's mind grasped at the name. Joe Stull! He was one of the best *sabreurs* in the country, it was said, though Wentworth had never crossed blades with him. A sudden suspicion flashed through his mind. Whoever had robbed the bank had evidently prepared in advance a place in the building where he could change clothing. Also, Stull was well-known about police headquarters and visited there frequently, having a passion for amateur dabbling in crime.

Wentworth jerked open the door. A redheaded police clerk jerked up a startled face.

"Has Mr. Joseph Stull been here today?" Wentworth demanded.

"Yes, sir," the clerk said. "He was here early this morning just after the commissioner left. He asked me to get some information from the Missing Persons Bureau. Was it all right, sir?"

Wentworth's lips began to twist in a small, tight smile.

"You left him alone in the outer office?"

The policeman's red head nodded slowly, face alarmed. "Wasn't it all right, sir?" he asked again.

"That was just fine," said Wentworth, and turned back to Holland and Kirkpatrick. He was smiling.

"I suggest," he said, "that you get Joe Stull's fingerprints and compare them with those on the operating lever in Elevator 5 at the bank!"

CHAPTER 7
MYSTERIOUS ATTACK

HOLLAND'S EYES were excited, but he shook his head quickly. "Stull sounds like he's worth checking on, but those fingerprints are no go," he said. "We took prints off the lever and they're all the operator's."

"All?" Wentworth queried, brows rising. "Then our friend the Fly must have worn gloves when he dropped the car to the third floor under our noses."

Holland shrugged. "He was clever enough about the rest of the affair. Here are a couple of things you don't know. The operator of Car 5 wasn't dead. We revived him, but he couldn't help us. Skull fracture. Also we found the Fly's clothes and the money sack in the street, thrown out a window apparently."

Wentworth frowned down at the platinum dial of his watch. "Those prints on the lever. Weren't they smeared?"

Holland shook his head. "All clear."

Wentworth's gray eyes narrowed slightly. He shrugged. "We've just time for cocktails before dinner," he said. "Join me, Kirk? Holland?"

Kirkpatrick shook his head. His only nephew, Corcoran, was awaiting him. The boy was just back from Heidelberg and Wentworth thought grimly that Kirkpatrick's resignation would cloud an otherwise very joyous reunion.

"Why don't you and Corkie join Nita and me later?" he suggested. "We're going to the Marlborough for some dancing."

Kirkpatrick looked up at him quickly, seeking in Wentworth's eyes some reason for the insistence. He found nothing there.

"I'll call you at Nita's," he said slowly.

Wentworth nodded and Holland walked out with him. They had chatted their way to within a block of the Tavern when Wentworth's ever-alert senses flashed him a warning. He jerked his head about. A racily streamlined sedan was lounging toward them. It was moving slowly, but its motor was roaring. Wentworth guessed the reason. The car was ready for a quick getaway, and that meant....

The thoughts were like a flash. Wentworth's actions were even swifter. He flung himself to the sidewalk, kicking Holland's feet out from under him. The two men sprawled to the pavement together, and instantly the peace of the dying day was ripped to shreds by the chattering snarl of a machine gun!

The second Wentworth hit the sidewalk he flung himself, rolling, toward the curb. His automatic sprang to his hand. The idling sedan was almost opposite now, roar of motor half drowning the drumroll of fire. The muzzle of the machine gun glinted in the window beside the car's rear seat. Even as Wentworth spotted it, the assassin jerked to his feet to depress the muzzle, to riddle his prostrate prey.

Wentworth checked his swift roll with an outflung hand. He snapped up his automatic and threw four bullets with trip-hammer speed into the car. The machine gunner stiffened convulsively. His murder weapon tilted toward the heavens and a buzzing stream of lead pocked the brick wall of a tenement.

At Wentworth's leap toward the running board, the driver of the sedan hurled the car forward. It pivoted a corner with a shriek of hot rubber. As it swished from sight Wentworth caught one more glimpse of the machine gunner. The man pitched backward, hands clawing at his lead-pierced breast.

Wentworth sprang to the center of the street for a taxi. A truck was waddling up the narrow passage between parked cars with more machines crawling behind it. By the time it had

ROSETTA DULAIN

DEPUTY
COMMISSIONER
HOLLAND

CHIEF INSPECTOR
MacTIVISH

The ? Fly

FRED
COOK

JOE
STULL

blundered clear…. Wentworth shrugged, holstered his automatic, and turned back to the sidewalk.

Holland sat with legs spread out awkwardly, a ridiculously startled look on his face. The few other persons on the street seemed still not to have grasped the meaning of that swift exchange of bullets. A man sat tilted back in a chair at a curb staring wildly over a spread-out newspaper. The man lost his balance and plunged into the gutter with frantic arms waving.

A slow smile twisted Wentworth's mouth as he helped Holland to his feet.

The Deputy Commissioner swallowed loudly and the blood receded from his fresh-complexioned cheeks. He wavered, rubber-kneed, over to the tenement wall and leaned his forehead against it. His body jerked.

SOMEWHERE ABOVE them a child was screaming with fright. An Italian woman thrust her fat face out a window and poured invective down upon the two men. Wentworth, grinning, shouted back in the idiom and the woman slammed down her window. He took Holland's arm and led him the block that remained to the Tavern. Police followed them there and got the details of the attack. When it was over, Holland turned an earnest face to Wentworth.

"I owe you my life," he said seriously.

Wentworth grinned. "Buy me a drink and we'll call it even," he said. "That was just as close a call for me as it was for you."

He was convinced that the machine gunner had sought to kill him, not Holland. He suspected the Fly had identified the Spider and was behind the attack. Yet he believed the Fly a shrewd amateur, rather than an ally of gangsters. And that machine gunner was a gangster, he knew, a killer attached to Fred Cook, smooth racketeer who, ostensibly, had gone legitimate since repeal.

Wentworth's eyes narrowed abruptly at a new thought. Why must the Fly necessarily be allied with Fred Cook? Could not Cook himself be the Fly, turning to a new pursuit now that liquor profits were reduced—and taxed? With a sense of sharp and important discovery, Wentworth recalled abruptly that Fred Cook had his headquarters in the Marlborough! It was to that hotel that the Fly had sent Rosetta Dulain!

Once more waving aside Holland's gratitude, Wentworth hastened to dress and go to the Marlborough. Nothing unusual happened and yet it seemed to Wentworth, enjoying a leisurely dinner with Nita, that an air of tension overlay the severely plain dining room with its murals of nudes endlessly pursuing nudes. For one thing, within five minutes of their entrance, a darkly grave man had taken a table nearby, a man with a splendidly athletic figure, with ironic dark eyes: Joseph Stull, the banker toward whom circumstances pointed as the Fly!

He dined alone with scarcely a glance for other occupants of the room. Yet his head movements were quick and twice he dropped a fork. Wentworth watched him secretly, but nothing developed, and when the dinner was half over, Kirkpatrick's nephew Corcoran joined them, presenting his uncle's apologies. He bowed with perfect heel-clicking poise, a blond boy with solemn eyes and a serious mien.

Nita welcomed him charmingly, her deep blue eyes bantering. "You've grown so adult, Corkie," she cried. "And you've even brought back a sword wound from Heidelberg. Tell me about it at once."

Corcoran laughed easily, fingering a thin white scar across his left cheek. "I came here tonight especially to meet the man who gave it to me," he said. "Lad named Friedrich Koch. You probably know him as Fred Cook. He slashed my cheek while I was attempting to disjoint his shoulder." He grimaced. "I didn't even touch his shoulder."

Wentworth's eyes sharpened as the significance of Corcoran's information struck home. Fred Cook, a gangster, was an expert with the sabres! That had been one item that had worried him in his speculation that the Fly and Cook might be one. And now that obstacle to the theory was also removed.

There were definitely two suspects now, Stull and Cook, both swordsmen, both with ample opportunity to commit the crimes in question, and both on the scene of impending action!

The slow smile that came to Wentworth's lips was gay. Action impended, yes, and either way it developed, Cook or Stull, it looked as if Spider and Fly would meet again tonight—with sabres!

Weighing the evidence against the two suspects, he absent-ly watched Nita and Corcoran chatting together, Nita's bronze-gleaming curls close to the boy's smooth blond hair. The heads turned and he sensed a general turning of attention toward the door. He spotted the cause with a swift uptake in his heartbeats. Here was the spark that would touch off action. Rosetta Dulain was entering the dining room!

Alone, and in a daringly cut gown of ivory satin, with her crown of flaming hair piled high, she was a figure to catch every eye. Wentworth saw that Corcoran's glance was amused.

"Effective," Corcoran commented drily, "but a bit spectacular."

Across his gaze Wentworth's eyes met Nita's, and he nodded almost imperceptibly. This was the woman they would watch. This was the woman about whose fiery head centered the storm gathering here tonight....

A SHARP exclamation from Corcoran pulled their attention from the woman. The boy's fingers were pressing sharply on Nita's arm. "Oh, I say!" he cried softly. *"There's* a beauty! Good Lord! It's... it's Ginnie!"

He was on his feet before Wentworth could stop him and striding across the room, headed straight for the table where a petite blonde had wrapped enthusiastic arms about Rosetta Dulain's carefully powdered throat. A man in evening dress stood just behind her, a man with dark waved hair. He twirled a monocle on a black ribbon.

"The man with the monocle," said Wentworth softly, "is Fred Cook. His machine gunner tried to kill me today."

As he spoke, Corcoran strode directly up to Dulain's table. The blonde girl whirled toward him, face startled, hand rising to a slender throat. Cook screwed the monocle into his eye and touched Corcoran on the shoulder peremptorily.

His face was plainly angry and for an instant the supercharged atmosphere of the dining room seemed literally to spark with increased tension. Wentworth half rose to his feet.

Corcoran turned slowly to face Cook. He ducked a stiffly correct bow, then straightened and touched the scar on his cheek. He was smiling. Cook stared at him, then abruptly laughed and clapped him on the shoulder. He turned toward the woman with a suave gesture.

Wentworth dropped back into his seat, leaning across the table. "Corcoran evidently recalled that affair at Heidelberg just in time," he said, "but something tells me that fireworks will start popping any moment now. Unless I miss my guess badly, that blonde is Rosetta Dulain's kid sister whom the Fly threatened. She came in with Fred Cook—and that is another link between Herr Koch and the Fly!"

Nita's eyes were worried, but her lips remained casually smiling.

"What are you going to do, Dick?" she asked quickly, and there was a catch in her breath. Her hand reached across the table and caught Dick's lean, strong fingers. She knew all the details of the affair with the Fly, knew to what life the Spider had committed himself. On occasion she joined him in his work. It was their one happiness, working together, for marriage was not for them.

What man would build a home, would bring children into the world when he knew death and disgrace threatened every hour of the day in his battles with the Underworld? There was only the joy of duty well-done, of thankless service to humanity amid terrific labors and peril. In these fine persons was no swerving from the path of duty, but sometimes, as now when her sweet blue eyes held his, there must be pain.

Wentworth smiled into those blue eyes, raised her white hand to his lips gently. Then, laughing, he got to his feet. No need to worry Nita in advance with the risks he must take.

"I'm just going to ask a few questions about our friend Cook," he said. "I've had my man on watch since I found Ma'amselle Dulain was coming here."

Nita's gaze grew more worried, but she fought her feelings with a smile. Wentworth felt his heart swell within him. Each time he left Nita, it was with the knowledge that it might be the last time he ever beheld her, that death might close his eyes forever on that vision of loveliness. His lips pressed together as he gazed at her, the warmth of her rounded shoulders above the simple caress of her delicate blue gown; the way that little lock of brown curled beside her ear... His fingers tightened on her hand.

"Dick!" Nita said sharply. "Dick, what is it?"

Dick bowed close, looking directly into her eyes and shaking his head slightly. "Mustn't look like that, dearest," he told her softly. "You wouldn't want to be kissed right out in public?"

A swift flush colored Nita's throat, stained her cheeks. "Dick!" she cried in confusion. "You'd do it, too!"

Wentworth nodded slowly, eyes caressing her. "Of course, darling."

Turning away, he laughed again, but hard, ugly glints replaced the caress in his eyes. There could be no sentiment for the Spider. There would be only the death-swift thrill of danger. If his man reported that Fred Cook alone had been to see Rosetta Dulain, it would indicate strongly that Cook and the Fly were one, and

Wentworth had sworn that the next time Spider and Fly met, one of them must die!

Wentworth wove a casual path among the tables, nodding now and again to acquaintances, took an elevator upward. The ninth floor was deep-carpeted and his careless feet were silent. A porter in blue dungarees stepped from a closet into his path and touched cupped hands to his forehead in a deep salaam. There was idolatry in his dark eyes when he looked up into Wentworth's face. For the porter was actually Ram Singh, his faithful Hindu body servant!

"Who has seen or talked to the woman?" Wentworth asked hurriedly in Hindustani.

He felt a tension in his body, a slow throbbing of his pulses in his throat. Ram Singh's answer might well point the way to the Fly!

"Two men," Ram Singh replied softly. "*Sahib* MacTivish of the police—and Fred Cook!"

MacTivish! But he had only sought more information from Rosetta about the Spider, of course—and Fred Cook!

Wentworth's lips curved in a small, cold smile.

"You have done well, Ram Singh," he said softly. "Keep up the watch. Meantime, in the next three quarters of an hour, make these phone calls. Use my name and try to locate *Sahib* Holland."

He handed Ram Singh a slip of paper, then pivoted and returned, unseen, to the fifth floor. Fred Cook's quarters were there….

CHAPTER 8
SABRES RING AGAIN

WENTWORTH DESCENDED to the fifth floor by the stairs. At the door of Cook's suite he fitted on a skirted mask which concealed his entire face. He thrust open the door and, automatic in hand, sprang into the room.

One man was within. He lunged forward out of a deep chair, fumbling for a weapon. His face was frightened, stunned, as he realized he could not draw in time. He froze in a crouch and stared at the masked man who held him imperturbably at gun point.

"Go to the phone," Wentworth ordered calmly. "Call Cook and tell him someone wants to see him on business in his rooms."

The man hesitated, crossed toward the phone, eyes shining with cunning. As he reached the instrument, Wentworth jammed the cold muzzle of his automatic against the man's nape.

"No tricks," he said curtly. "This gun kills."

The rigidity of the man's neck was a greater assurance of obedience than his hoarse plea for mercy. His hand trembled as he plucked the receiver from a wall phone and husked Wentworth's message into the transmitter.

As he talked, Wentworth's eyes skipped about the room. It was sparsely furnished, but upon the wall a beautiful pair of sabres was crossed. A smile touched his hidden lips.

When the man replaced the receiver, Wentworth tapped him behind the ear with the gun muzzle. The man fell, and in thirty seconds was bound and gagged. Wentworth took the sabres from the wall and slid them across a table in the center of the room. He stepped behind the door then and, gun in hand, waited for the Fly—and a duel to the death!

Ten minutes passed before Wentworth heard the careless rasp of the doorknob. He placed his left hand against the door and, when it had swung wide, thrust it briskly. It clapped shut. Wentworth leaped forward... and caught his breath with a curse. Two men had entered the room, and one was Corcoran!

"Hands up, both of you," Wentworth jerked out. "Careful, Cook, a gun's on your back."

The dapper gang leader lifted his hands to shoulder height and twisted his dark impassive face about. He smiled ironically at the mask. "Better do as he says, Corcoran, old top," Cook drawled. "This man is an amateur and they're apt to be dangerous."

"Excellent advice," Wentworth drawled in the flat, mocking tones of the Spider. "If Mr. Corcoran will march straight forward ten paces...."

"Go ahead," Cook urged.

Wentworth could see an angry rush of blood reddening Corcoran's neck. He felt his liking for him mount. A plucky youngster he was, and Wentworth hoped he wouldn't make it necessary to strike him, but the Fly was too smooth a man to take chances with. He lifted the gun barrel slightly.

"Do what he says," Cook said urgently, "or he'll knock you out and you'll miss all the fun."

Corcoran hesitated a moment longer, then strode forward

ten full paces and pivoted toward his host and captor. His face was tight with anger.

"Now, Cook," said Wentworth softly. "As you see, there are two sabres—your own—upon the table. It is my intention to duel you."

Corcoran frowned. Cook turned about slowly. His face was puzzled too, but there was unmistakable mockery there.

"Delighted!" he exclaimed. "But may I first know the identity of my opponent?"

Wentworth nodded slowly. He flicked a swift glance over the room to fix the location of furniture in his mind. The man he had knocked out and bound was stirring now. By his head was the door to a bedroom. Behind Wentworth was another door, leading into the third room of the suite. The chamber in which the three stood was sparsely furnished, chairs along the wall, the table in the center.

"Yes," said Wentworth softly, still in mocking accents. "If you do not already know, I will tell you. Your opponent is—*the Spider!*"

Corcoran let out a low exclamation of surprise. Cook's breath sucked in and mockery fled from his face.

"You have asked for a duel," he said slowly, "and I will not refuse. But may I know why the Spider seeks me out? I may have transgressed in the past, but at present I do nothing to earn your animosity. Understand, I do not seek to avoid the affair, but I am curious…." His voice raised slightly. "Very well, I can see you do not intend to answer. Let us fight *now!*"

AS HE spoke the last word, he sprang swiftly backward toward a chair. Wentworth heard the opening of a door behind him and pitched to the floor. As he dropped, he heard a whisper of some missile hissing above him, heard Cook gasp in pain and surprise.

"Don't shoot, Spider," came a gentle voice. "I do not now seek your life, but my gun is ready."

Wentworth, rolling to bring his automatic to bear, flopped over on his back—and stared into the muzzle of an air pistol whose deadliness he recognized. He looked above it into the smiling, unmasked face above, into black eyes half masked by heavy lids, merry beneath smooth blond brows.

"*The Fly!*" he exclaimed.

The smile became mockingly deferential. "As our friend Cook might say," said the Fly, "it seems to be amateur night."

Wentworth sat up and, without use of his hands, rose dexterously to his feet. He let his gun hang idly at his side. The Fly stood alone in an opened doorway, but on the floor of the lighted room beyond, Wentworth made out the supine bodies of two men. He did not need the glittering pools of crimson to tell him they were dead, to tell him that the Fly had prevented the Spider from being shot in the back when Cook cried his signal, "now."

He turned casually and saw that Cook sprawled upon his back, a knife hilt protruding from his chest, a hilt that terminated in a fly-shaped knob of gold! Corcoran seemed dazed by the swiftness of events. Beneath the skirted mask, Wentworth's face was puzzled.

"It seems," he said slowly, "that I owe my life to you, Fly, though I am at a loss to understand the reason you saved me."

The Fly smiled negligently and Wentworth studied his face seeking some identifying feature. Was this man Joe Stull?

"Noblesse oblige, Spider," the Fly said lightly. "You spared me when you might have run a sabre through my heart. I cannot do less. But next time, Spider, next time we meet it will be with sabres to the death!"

Wentworth waved a hand toward the swords. "There's no time like the present," he said.

The Fly laughed. "Sorry, Spider, there are too many possibilities of interruption. But I shall not forget."

He sprang back sharply, jerked shut the door. Wentworth leaped to the hall exit, but ducked aside at the swift beat of feet behind him. He whirled to face a sabre in Corcoran's hand. The boy's young face was flushed with excitement, the sabre scar upon his cheek a scarlet line. He held the sword poised before him expertly.

"Get your sabre, Spider," he challenged.

"Don't be a fool," Wentworth snapped. "That man is the one who robbed the bank today!"

He could see the words made no impression upon Corcoran. The boy was between him and the door. The Fly was escaping. But, short of shooting, Wentworth could not get past that naked, menacing blade. He cursed, snatched the other blade from the table.

Corcoran laughed with excitement. *"En garde!"* he called eagerly.

Wentworth fell into position and feinted twice like lightning. Corcoran's blade followed swiftly. There was a clash, a ring of steel, and the boy's sabre glittered across the room, struck the floor on its point, and swayed like a flower on its flexible blade. Wentworth darted for the door. Corcoran sprang at him and snatched the mask.

It ripped clear, but in the instant before his face was bared, Wentworth smashed a bullet into the ceiling light. The sound of the shot crashed thunderously against the walls. Men and police would come on the run now, but there had been no other way. Wentworth wrenched open the door, hurled Corcoran into the hall, clapped the door shut again.

He crossed swiftly to the windows, climbed to the sill. Lowering the casement again, he toed along the narrow ledge that girded the Marlborough at the fifth floor. Two minutes later the Spider opened a door quietly and slipped into the hall from a fire escape. Three minutes after that Richard Wentworth sauntered among the tabled guests of the dining room and dropped into a chair beside Nita.

He glanced casually about. With narrowing eyes he saw Joseph Stull was no longer at his table! The Dulain woman and the blonde girl had vanished too. When Corcoran, face still flushed, came back to the table, Wentworth was quietly sipping his wine. He listened with appropriate comment to the boy's excited account of the encounter of the Spider and the Fly, examined the captured mask curiously.

Wentworth sighed, lifted his wine glass and smiled with his

eyes into Nita's reproving gaze. "Some people have all the fun," said Wentworth regretfully. "Nothing ever happens to me."

CHAPTER 9
THE MENACE GROWS

WENTWORTH GLANCED up to find Holland and Inspector MacTivish striding directly toward them across the room. He spoke to Nita without moving his lips. "Cut it," he said swiftly. "Here come police. Corcoran, if they ask you specifically, you'll have to talk. Otherwise, save it for Kirk."

He pretended then to see Holland and MacTivish for the first time and got courteously to his feet as they came near. "Hello," he called gaily. "What excuse have you for putting the Marlborough on your expense account?"

Holland's blond brows were drawn down tightly over his eyes. "The Fly's at work here," he said abruptly, "and this gentleman with you was seen leaving the room where the Fly killed three men. I'll have to ask him to accompany us."

Wentworth smiled. "Allow me to introduce," he said, "Corcoran Kirkpatrick, only nephew and heir apparent to Commissioner Stanley Kirkpatrick."

Holland's face was startled. He jerked an apologetic bow. "But you were in that room, weren't you?" he demanded, and Inspector MacTivish's steady black eyes regarded Corcoran over his shoulder.

"I was," Corcoran said shortly, and detailed all that had occurred. MacTivish's black gaze switched to Wentworth, regarding him fixedly. Wentworth thought suddenly that his heavy-lidded black eyes were very like the Fly's....

"There are a number of curious things here," said Holland. "We have had a watch on the hotel for several hours, in fact, ever since one of our men followed Stull here and we learned that Rosetta Dulain was here, too. But the Fly has disappeared absolutely. No one saw him go."

Wentworth's eyes were not on Holland, but on MacTivish. Disappeared. Couldn't MacTivish, or Stull, if either was the Fly, merely change back to his true identity and walk out?

"Another thing I can't understand," Holland went on, "is the presence of this envelope on Cook's body."

Wentworth looked at him then and saw a long manila envelope. He took it, and found inside fifteen thousand dollars in large denomination bills. He examined the cancellation stamp and smiled abruptly into Holland's eyes, indicating it with a tapping finger.

"This letter is postmarked in the Hudson Terminal Post Office," he said, "the nearest to the Race National Bank. The time stamp is one o'clock; the robbery was at noon...."

Holland seized the envelope. "You mean this money was stolen from the bank?"

"It's a guess, of course, but I think an accurate one," said Wentworth. "This would explain, too, how the money was smuggled out of the building. The robber merely had addressed envelopes ready, went to the office where he changed clothes, and slipped the money into the envelopes. If we had looked in the mail box while we were there, we would have recovered the entire million!"

A slip of paper fluttered from the envelope and Wentworth stooped and picked it up. He was thinking abruptly that Mac-Tivish or Stull might very well have mailed the money and resumed his true identity in the bank. Search there had been futile, too. He glanced at MacTivish and found hatred in the inspector's eyes!

Wentworth read the slip aloud:

> Easy money, eh? This is part of the loot of the Race Nation-
> al. If you want more easy money, wait for word from—
>   THE FLY.

His face became grim. "Don't you see what this means, Holland?" he demanded. "It means the Fly is planning to unite every criminal element in the city in one gigantic organization! He's baiting them with gifts of money. If Fred Cook, big man that he was in the underworld, got only fifteen thousand of a million loot, how many men got these letters and these provocative notes?"

Holland stared at him, wide-eyed. "Good Lord!" It was a whisper.

"The thing to do," said Wentworth, "is to put a trail on every notorious criminal and try to get a clue to the Fly through them."

"Nonsense," MacTivish cut in. "Wentworth is just trying to turn us aside from the main issue. He probably dropped that note himself. Listen, Mr. Wentworth, when the Spider was in Cook's rooms, where were you?"

WENTWORTH STARED at him fixedly. Was this further proof that MacTivish was the Fly? Did he know the Spider's true identity and was he striking at him in this way? Wentworth's lips smiled coldly, though he felt the pulse of danger in the scar upon his temple. None of what he felt showed in his face.

"I was waiting for you to ask me that, MacTivish," he said gently. "Believe it or not, I was in a telephone booth waiting for a streetcar."

MacTivish snorted and began to hammer at him on that point, and Wentworth quietly signaled for his check. When it was brought to him, he tossed it upon the table. Upon it were entered the charges for six telephone calls, the numbers and time of each call, covering the half hour when Wentworth had been absent from the table.

The inspector's sharp-nosed face showed obvious disappointment. He whirled on Corcoran. "Why didn't you call police about those killings?" he demanded.

Corcoran was on his feet now, glowering his young dislike into the police inspector's face. "I was consulting Mr. Wentworth on the best procedure," he said. "He had just advised me to call the police when you two gentlemen came to the table."

Wentworth uttered a mental cheer for Corcoran, but his face was grave and his manner chilling as he got to his feet. "This has gone on long enough," he said coldly. "You know where to reach any of us if you need further information. Pardon me." He thrust MacTivish aside and circled the table to assist Nita with her wrap. It was black taffeta and its ruffled bottom swept the floor disdainfully as she led the way across the dining room, followed by Wentworth and the still angry Corcoran.

In Wentworth's Lancia, with the broad shouldered Jackson behind the wheel, Corcoran turned to Wentworth. "Why," he wanted to know, "did MacTivish want to know where you had been when I told them I'd seen the Spider?"

Wentworth passed cigarettes to Nita and to Corcoran, lighting all three before he replied. "It is a little obsession of the police," he said casually, smiling at the glowing tip of his cigarette. "It happens that in my criminal investigation work I have appeared at the same times and places as the Spider, and one or the other of us has beaten the police to their capture quite often. Naturally"—he snapped the flame out of his lighter, leaned back comfortably on the velvet cushions—"Naturally, such things pique their vanity."

Nita said wearily, "I get so tired of hearing about this Spider. Corcoran, tell me about that little blonde beauty you rushed."

Corcoran stammered in the darkness and Wentworth laughed silently.

WHEN, A half hour later, Wentworth opened the door of his apartment, a redheaded woman in a close ivory gown rushed up to him and threw both arms about his neck.

"Dick, Dick!" she cried. "The Fly has stolen Ginnie!"

Wentworth unfolded her arms with deft hands and thrust her back a careful three feet. It was Rosetta Dulain and her face was stained with the tracery of tears.

"My dear lady!" he exclaimed. "This is really very distressing, but who in the devil are you?"

Corcoran thrust past Wentworth, seized the woman by the shoulders. "What did you say?" he demanded hoarsely. "What did you say?"

The woman was still staring distractedly at Wentworth. His face was amused, but he was far from entertained. How in the name of heaven had this woman found out his identity? If she had not learned that the Spider and Richard Wentworth were one, why was she here? He turned toward Nita and shrugged slightly.

Her own face was as smiling as his own. "Did you invite the lady here, Corcoran?" she asked.

Rosetta Dulain's frightened eyes pulled from Wentworth's face to that of the blond boy. She seized the satin lapels of Corcoran's dinner jacket in frantic hands.

"Please, please," she said. "Help me find Ginnie."

Corcoran patted her shoulder, whirled toward Wentworth. "Can't you help, Mr. Wentworth?" he pleaded. "The girl she's talking about is the girl we saw with her at the Marlborough. It's her sister, Ginnie Clark."

Wentworth raised his mildly mocking brows. Nita repeated her question as to whether the boy had asked Rosetta to the apartment. Corcoran shook his head, worried eyes still appealing to Wentworth.

"I'll tell you," Rosetta broke in, thrusting past him. "The Fly told me to come here. He said I must wait my chance and betray you into his hands, tell him all your plans, or he would—he would—" The woman sank to the floor, shoulders and fiery head sagging. She raised her hands to her face and rocked backward and forward, sobbing, "Ginnie… Ginnie… Ginnie."

Wentworth looked down sympathetically on the broken woman. "I still don't know what it's all about," he said slowly, "but see what you can do for her, Nita."

He helped Rosetta to her feet and she tottered like a weak old woman. Nita took her in charge and Wentworth walked on into his music room, frowning at the floor, hands clasped behind him. The woman obviously was telling the truth. The Fly had penetrated his identity. Wentworth shrugged. That did not necessarily follow. The man was clever enough to send the woman here in an attempt to trap him into admitting he was the Spider.

Well, the Fly had failed in that, but also he had made it impossible for Wentworth to use Rosetta Dulain as a spy. Perhaps he could still make a bargain that if he rescued the sister Ginnie… Wentworth was conscious of Corcoran's distraught presence. The boy was standing woodenly by the door, watching his silent pacing.

Wentworth turned and smiled slowly at him. "We'll do what we can, Corcoran," he promised, "though I still do not see why the woman was sent here unless the Fly is laboring under the same misapprehension as the police."

Corcoran came forward slowly. "For God's sake, Mr. Wentworth," he pleaded, "save Ginnie. I—I love her."

Wentworth stared fixedly at him. "Rather sudden, isn't it, Corcoran?" he asked kindly.

Wentworth, half dazed, sprang with all his might for the victoria.

Corcoran shook his head violently. "I've been loving her for three years," he said. "I saw her in a convent in France once and…. Well, she was moved elsewhere and I never saw her again. I've been dreaming of her ever since."

It was all clear now. Rosetta Dulain had placed her sister in a French convent with strict orders that she be allowed no friends from outside. And when she had been informed of Corcoran's interest, she had moved the girl. It was apparent the Fly had located Rosetta's sister and brought her to America.

Wentworth clapped his hand on his shoulder. "It's all right, old man. We'll save Ginnie," he said.

Corcoran sank into a chair, his face in his hands. "When I think of Ginnie in the hands of that fiend!"

Wentworth glanced longingly toward his violin, toward the mighty organ that filled one end of the duplex room. He was a past master of both instruments, but there was no time now to seek solace in music. He spun on his heel and sought the room where Nita had taken Rosetta.

Rosetta Dulain sat limply in an armchair, her fiery head lolling backward, eyes closed. Her face, devoid of makeup, was almost transparently white. Nita sat quietly by.

The woman had opened her shadowed eyes at his first word and she looked at him without lifting her heavy head. "I am afraid to talk," she said simply. "If you are not the Spider, it would do no good. The Spider is the only man who can beat the Fly."

Wentworth pretended anger. "The Spider and I have fought the same man before this," he said shortly. "Sometimes he wins;

sometimes I beat him to the criminal. I do not concede that the Spider is the better man."

The woman eyed him fixedly; then slowly her eyes shut again. "I'll have to think," she said, almost as if talking to herself. "I may have to ask your help. I know nowhere else to go. But the Spider—" her voice trailed off and Wentworth wondered if she were recalling the escape the Spider had staged in her apartment. "You must give me time to think," she repeated. "If I talk at all, I risk terrible things for Ginnie. But if I don't, God knows what will be the end of her—and for me."

Her voice died in inexpressible weariness and Nita quietly drew Wentworth from the room.

"I think she'll talk," she breathed into his ear. "Leave her to me."

Wentworth smiled and put his arms about Nita, looking down into her lovely face, the warm eyes raised to his. This was one of the few moments that Fate—was it in pity?—allowed these two who loved so greatly, so unselfishly. Tomorrow, within the hour, death's cold hand might separate them, but this one moment....

Corcoran, stepping then into the half darkened hall, saw and smiled sadly, thinking of another love, and silently tiptoed away....

CHAPTER 10
A FLY CAN KILL

MORNING SUNLIGHT fell dazzlingly on the gilded finery of Fifth Avenue. The early cool was swallowed in swooning heat, but not even August could stop the pulse of life through this artery of the world's elite. August could not, but presently the Fly would....

North of the bustle of the roaring Forties, beyond the jostling skyscrapers with their human ants, Fifth Avenue becomes quiet and rich, as brown water that dances past rapids glides smoothly into the gracious stillness of deep pools. Traffic still swirls past grand portals, green double-deck buses, and fender scraping taxis of myriad hues, but even its raucous note seems subdued, awed by the hauteur of wealth.

It was not often the fleshless jaws of tragic death grinned there, unless a playing urchin lurched beneath crushing wheels— and few urchins penetrated here.

Today death would grin here, would even laugh!

From the press of traffic, now and again a suave foreign car noses its bullet-shaped bonnet to the curb before a shop; a liveried footman springs to the door and a woman sedately crosses a canopied walk. It was such a car that the Fly occupied, a wine-colored Renault, at ease behind a chauffeur, as he surveyed the camp that was Fifth Avenue and reflected complacently on the competence of his planning.

At one point he leaned forward and stared intently. A low-swung truck bearing a safe was backed to the curb and a crew of men was preparing to hoist the vault into a building. It all looked innocent enough....

Up the broad thoroughfare a little way, discreet shops gave way to soaring apartment houses that overlooked the cool greenery of Central Park. There, where the residential merged into the trade, stood the Plaza Hotel, aloof behind its formal square of parkland and statuary.

As his Renault rolled past the hotel, the Fly's careless, lid-veiled eyes lighted on the familiar horse-drawn cabs in line by the park, and his lips twitched in a smile. Horses whose coats glistened with the sheen of patient grooming were hitched to gleaming victorias. There was even a lone hansom. The drivers, resplendent in the plug-hatted garb of thirty years ago, stood carelessly by, whips in hand.

The smile touched the Fly's lips with mockery. As his Renault neared this last stand of the nineties, he tapped upon the glass with his cane and the landau slid to the curb. A drive through the park while Death laughed above Fifth Avenue? Why not? Affairs were arranged to his liking. Those provocative little notes mailed out with gifts of loot from the Race National had borne fruit. The sack of Fifth Avenue was only one of a half dozen robberies his fertile brain had mapped for the day, and he had half a hundred men eager to do his bidding. Why not a leisurely drive through the park?

He raised his cane to a cabbie and, debonairly smiling, began a peaceful circuit of the driveways behind the smart cropping of hoofs while curious motorists scooting past stared in scornful envy. The Fly was not disguised; that is, he had the same features, the same amused, dark-eyed stare that the Spider had seen and that two other men had remarked, briefly, before they died.

The Fly thought for a moment of the Spider. He had another little enterprise that would tie that worthy's hands…. Later they would meet again with the sabres. The Fly tapped his neatly shod foot with his cane. He was well pleased with himself.

Richard Wentworth was distinctly not satisfied with himself. Cantering through the same park the Fly was circling in his victoria, Wentworth frowned at his horse's ears. His early morning ride had been delayed. Nita's confidence that Rosetta Dulain would talk had not been fulfilled, despite several hours of intense questioning.

Wentworth had checked on several angles by telephone. Holland had not been available, but through Kirkpatrick he had ascertained that neither Stull nor MacTivish had an alibi for the period of the Fly's activities. But then, neither had the Spider.

There was nothing to point conclusively to either man. Mac-Tivish had been in the neighborhood of the Race National on another matter at the time of the holdup, and when the first police arrived, they found him on the scene. Practically the same thing was true of Stull. Wentworth realized that he must force Rosetta Dulain to talk if he was to run the Fly to earth, if he was to thwart the huge organization the man was building. If Wentworth could have known to what degree that organization already was perfected, if he could have known what threatened on Fifth Avenue….

WENTWORTH WAS circling southward at a sharp canter now, at a place in the West Eighties where the bridle path skirted the automobile drive. The wind was in his face, bringing not the fresh odors of growing things beneath the sun, but the heavy fumes of gasoline exhausts. Abruptly he jerked up his head, listening. There it was again! Good Lord, it couldn't be! But he knew it was! The chattering horror of machine guns— machine guns on Fifth Avenue!

Wentworth jabbed home his spurs, slapped his crop on the horse's flank. His bay mare reared in astonishment, pawing the air with her forehoofs; then, as spurs jabbed again, she leaped forward in a startled bound and tore down the bridle path at full gallop!

Low on his horse's neck, Wentworth calculated swiftly. The path wound a leisurely way toward Central Park West.

A half mile ahead and to his left lay one of the scattered lakes of the park. Between him and Fifth Avenue were rocky grades, thick-growing trees.... Abruptly Wentworth hauled the bay back on its haunches, threw it into the auto driveway, luckily clear of cars for the moment. Its shoes struck suddenly on the sun-softened asphalt. A few hundred feet ahead was the Seventy-seventh Street crosscut that burrowed between stone walls straight across the park. If the horse could make the jump to the cross-cut—

Just ahead of him a victoria made its leisurely trotting way, a silk-hatted man lolling on the cushions. As the furious beat of Wentworth's gallop rang out, the man turned and stared backward. His face was but a pale blur in the bright sunlight to Wentworth. Then, suddenly, his attention focused sharply on the man. For the victoria's driver turned a startled face; his whip swished and the victoria lurched swaying behind a galloping horse!

Wentworth stared hard at the man, then sucked in his breath hissingly. It was the Fly! And those machine guns on Fifth Avenue—Here was the man who was responsible!

The fact that he was unarmed did not deter Wentworth. He crouched lower on the mare's neck, lashing violently. A mounted policeman on the bridle path, now a full fifty yards from the drive and dipping to pass under it, spotted the fantastic chase. His shrilling whistle bit a warning through the sunlit morning. Wentworth's mind registered the sound, recognized it—but that was all.

He was gaining now on the victoria, but not so swiftly as he had hoped. He had ridden hard that morning, and the mare had been dark with a lather of sweat before the chase had begun. The horse ahead was comparatively fresh.

Wentworth glanced swiftly toward the policeman, saw him spurring up the grade toward them. That was slow riding. Before he could intercept, the victoria would dash across that bridge across the Seventy-seventh Street crosscut just ahead. And the policeman would be in the rear, trailing Wentworth.

The mounted officer apparently realized that fact even as Wentworth did, for he fired a shot into the air. A short laugh barked from Wentworth's lips. Little did that cop know that he was attempting to frighten the most daring men of modern annals, the Fly and the Spider!

Then Wentworth saw his chance. Ahead, the road curved widely in a great circuit to the left. The terrain of the bow was impossible for riding, but if he jumped the lined benches, he would have the inside of the track. As he threw the mare from the road to the walk, sent it in a swift, easy bound over the benches, he caught the gleam of a gun in the Fly's hand.

But Wentworth's mare was flashing behind a line of shade trees now. Triumph gleamed in the Spider's eyes. The Fly would be between himself and the policeman. He would be forced either to remain in the victoria—in which case he must come to grips with the Spider; or he must take to the woods on foot—and there would be two mounted men to pursue!

Gauging the speed of the victoria, Wentworth calculated that at the climax of the curve, his mare and the victoria would be racing side by side. He urged the horse on with spur and whip and voice. In moments now, in little moments….

HE FLASHED into the last fifty-foot dash, saw the Fly's victoria just ahead, the terrified driver lashing his horse. Then, from the victoria, a gun blasted. Wentworth felt the horse beneath him spring wildly forward and upward as the bullet caught it. He had barely time to kick his feet free of the stirrups when the mare spilled on its head, nose digging the walk, body flying high.

Wentworth balled himself expertly for the fall, pitched clear and rolled on his shoulders. He came to his feet, half-dazed, but springing with all the mighty power of his thighs for the victoria.

The Fly raised his gun again, sighting at the Spider's laboring chest. With a curse that was a sob, Wentworth hurled himself desperately to the earth. The lead whined harmlessly overhead. A succession of banging reports whipping past him, terrific rocking concussions that numbed the brain. Wentworth knew that somewhere near where the machine guns had blasted, a huge charge of explosives had let go. In his racing mind, he could glimpse the unutterable carnage that would cause on Fifth Avenue, and it was the Fly who was responsible!

On the instant, Wentworth was up again, racing toward the carriage. He saw the Fly settling back into his cushions, saw the victoria flash past, hopelessly beyond his reach. Jerking his head to the right, Wentworth saw why the Fly was no longer concerned.

The mounted policeman lay flat upon his back in the drive! The cop's horse stood, head hanging, nuzzling the body. Three autos, bunched at the curve, rounded into view and halted with a squealing of brakes. Wentworth sprinted toward them, shouting. Men sprang from two of them and hurried to the cop. Wentworth reached them moments later, snatched the policeman's gun and extra bullets.

"Take him to the hospital," he ordered one motorist. "Come on," he shouted to another. "The murderer is in a carriage down there, escaping."

The second driver was a youngster. "Right," he snapped and sprang to the wheel as Wentworth leaped to the running board. The car lurched forward, clashing through gear shifts. Wentworth wormed in between the forward mudguard and the hood of the car, reloading the policeman's half-emptied gun. The victoria was out of sight around the bend.

A short distance ahead, Wentworth knew the road branched, one part circling to the left about the lake, the other climbing a hill to the Seventy-second Street exit of the park.

Wentworth pointed up the hill and the car roared into it. At the crest they found the victoria. It was stationary and the driver was trembling upon his seat, staring straight ahead. The Fly was nowhere in sight. He had caught a taxi on Central Park West, the driver said hoarsely.

"I'm going to learn to drive a taxi," the man quavered. "I thought this was a nice, peaceful life, driving in the park, and here...."

His voice faded as the car raced out of the park, but there was no trace of the Fly. Wentworth caught a taxi and sent it toward Fifth Avenue. Shattered windows gaped everywhere. As they neared the Plaza, traffic was in unutterable confusion.

A policeman waved them aside, shook his head angrily, and bellowed at an attempt to argue the taxi through the lines. Wentworth pushed on afoot, elbowing through thick crowds. His card from Kirkpatrick got him past the final close cordon and he stopped abruptly, staring. He felt the street tilt crazily, felt the nausea of horror quiver in his vitals. For Fifth Avenue was a shambles.

A double-deck bus lay shattered upon its side and white-coated ambulance men labored beside the blue uniforms of police dragging pitiful bodies from its wreckage.

Other autos were strewn in an incredible tangle of bloody

wreckage across the street behind the rampart of a huge, low-swung truck such as is used for carrying safes. That was jammed directly across the avenue. The body of a woman had been wrapped around a lamppost like a torn and blood-soaked dishrag. Wentworth knew it was a woman because her hair was silvery and long.... In the crowd a man was retching with nausea.

Wentworth tore his eyes from the horror of the avenue and stared upward. A rig for hoisting safes protruded from the sixth story of a building that leaned like the Tower of Pisa and threatened momentarily to collapse into the avenue. The entire front had been blown away for a height of two stories and the steel support beams were twisted like the wires of a battered bird cage. A great hole gaped in the pavement. This, then, was the result of that terrific blast whose concussions had beaten upon him in the park.

WENTWORTH TURNED from all that death and gruffly asked details of a white-faced policeman. The man knew only fragments. An alarm to his precinct station had told of a holdup in an exclusive Fifth Avenue jeweler's shop. Reserves had sped to the scene and halfway there, the car had been wrecked by the blast. They had gone on afoot and found this.

Wentworth nodded slowly. He saw now what had been accomplished. That safe dangling in the air above the pavement had served a double purpose. It had kept people clear of that side of the street, had permitted the thieves to enter a store empty of customers. Perhaps they had killed the men within. No one would ever know now, thanks to the explosion. When they had fled, the safe had been left dangling with some device for severing the ropes after a short time and letting it crash to the street.

And the safe had been full of explosives!

The Fly had figured, and figured correctly, that the blast would blot out all pursuit, wipe out all possible clues to the bandits. Wentworth was willing to wager that the safe movers had a permit for the job and that it would be found men had fraudulently represented themselves as employees of a legitimate safe-moving firm.

Deputy Commissioner Holland—but it had been "Commissioner" since early that morning—jostled through the crowd to Wentworth's side, his blue eyes blazing. When he could talk, he told Wentworth that this was only a part of the day's atrocities.

"Three armored trucks are missing," he reported incisively. "We found one in the river, its crew all dead of gas. Phosgene is the doctor's guess. We found one witness of one holdup. He said the truck was hauled inside a big truck up a runway formed by the tailgate and was driven away. Two men with machine guns blazed away at every living thing on the street. There must have been fifty dead in those three attacks. By God," he swore violently, "I'll get the Fly before another day has passed, or die in the attempt!"

At his tense cry, Wentworth raised his head. "It is certain the Fly did it, then?"

Holland nodded heavily. "There was a note from the Fly in the armored truck that we recovered. He seems to have formed the organization he wanted."

Wentworth then related what had happened in the park and, after endless questions, made his way homeward along the shambles that once had been the proud and serene Fifth Avenue.

Nita met him at the door of his apartment and the bitterness of her blue eyes stopped him short on the threshold. His lips shut in a grim line.

"What now?" he asked quietly, though his heart thumped suffocatingly into his throat. Disaster was everywhere. Abruptly he knew that it had invaded his own home, too.

"Rosetta's sister phoned," Nita said swiftly. "Corkie recognized her voice. She said the Fly had her captive, and then a man cut in and Corkie went crazy. He said he had a clue and ran out of the house before I could stop him."

Wentworth's fists knotted at his sides. Corcoran gone on a chase like that, in answer to a call from the Fly. He had grown immensely fond of his friend's only nephew, grown to like the boy even as he admired and respected Kirkpatrick himself. He realized achingly what all this pointed to.

"Tell me the rest of it," he said between tight lips. "There is more, I know."

"Yes," said Nita slowly. "There is more. Corkie went away three hours ago. We haven't heard from him since. Twice a man has called and asked for you, a man whose voice I do not know. He won't talk to anyone but you."

"The Fly!" Wentworth ground out. He shook a clenched fist above his head. "The Fly has got Corcoran in his power!"

CHAPTER 11
THE FLY'S WARNING

NITA HALF shrank from the ferocity of Wentworth's expression as he realized that the Fly had kidnapped Corcoran Kirkpatrick, then she smiled and put a hand on his arm. Her smile was confident. "You'll save him, Dick, I know," she said. "You'll run the Fly to earth, too."

Cold anger had crept through Wentworth's veins to the fingertips. It battled with his despair of penetrating the incredibly clever operations of the super-criminal who this day had loosed death and destruction upon Fifth Avenue, who now had struck even in the home of the Spider!

"Is Dulain here?" Wentworth spoke between his teeth.

Nita's wide blue eyes searched his. "Yes," she replied hesitantly.

Wentworth nodded and strode down the dim hall and swung into the woman's room, stood rigidly just inside the door, tall in his riding garb. Rosetta Dulain lay wretchedly upon a chaise lounge twisted about so that she buried her face on bent arms. Her clothing was disarrayed, not subtly for allurement, but with the carelessness of a woman too sorrowing to notice.

"Get up," Wentworth ordered.

The woman flinched from his voice, jerked up a haggard face. The smudged shadows beneath her eyes made it gaunt.

"Get up!" Wentworth said again.

"I didn't do it," the woman protested. "I didn't!"

She swung her feet to the floor, reached up imploring hands. Wentworth's eyes continued to bore into hers.

"You entered this house by a trick," he said shortly. "You aroused young Corcoran's interest in your sister. When the Fly phoned, you begged Corcoran to go to her rescue, knowing he would be taken prisoner."

As the words pounded at her, Rosetta Dulain cringed away. She drew her feet under her and inched back into the farthest corner of the couch. Her eyes were horribly frightened.

"No," she pleaded. *"No!"*

"You came here to work treachery," Wentworth proceeded, relentless as a judge. "I was fool enough to think you were only worried about your sister. You have achieved that treachery. You shall atone for it, or—"

Fear shook the woman's disordered head, her tangled hair twirled about her shoulders. The flimsy negligee she wore, borrowed from Nita, was dragged from a shoulder. Wentworth leaned toward her, eyes cold.

His right hand shot out and gripped her naked shoulder, then snapped away and pointed where he had touched. There was a twisted smile on his mouth. New waves of terror convulsed the woman's face. Fearfully, she turned her head, but her eyes clung to Wentworth's. Finally, she jerked her gaze toward the white roundness of her shoulder. When she saw what was there, she screamed twice and slumped in a dead faint.

Wentworth, smiling grimly, reached out and removed from her shoulder a small Spider made of crimson wool and wire and dropped it in his vest pocket. He turned to Nita, wide-eyed in the doorway.

"Send Ram Singh," he requested briefly.

Nita turned away and presently the dark-faced Hindu slippered into the room. He was clad in the conventional white house costume and upon his head was a snowy, freshly wrapped turban.

"Come here, Ram Singh," Wentworth said softly, "and hold your knife naked in your hand."

The Hindu's dark eyes flashed. A knife with a nine-inch blade slid from his belt and he stood with it glittering before him. Wentworth massaged Rosetta's throat and forehead, and she opened terrified eyes, glanced swiftly to her shoulder. She clasped it with agonized fingers and stared up again.

"You'd better talk," said Wentworth. "Tell me all you know of the Fly, or it may be—the Spider shall touch your forehead!"

A cry began in the woman's throat. Her eyes flew to Ram Singh and his shining knife, and the cry died.

"I promised to find your sister and free her," Wentworth spoke on. "You repaid that by sending my friend into the trap of the Fly. I am still ready to fulfill my part of the bargain, but you must talk, or—" His hand started toward her again.

HOARSE WORDS chattered from the woman's mouth, words of fright, of dread of the Fly, of vengeance upon her sister; pleas for pardon, for protection, but ultimately she sank back exhausted, her body sagging in surrender.

"What do you want to know?" she agreed.

"First," said Wentworth. "Where is the Fly?"

Rosetta shook her head. "He always comes to me or sends messages."

"What did he say when you talked to him?"

"He wanted to know," the woman spoke slowly, "whether you were going to the opera tonight."

"The opera!" Wentworth stared down at her with narrowing eyes. Good Lord! Did the Fly plan at the opera some such depredation as this day had strewn Fifth Avenue with mangled human bodies? He questioned Rosetta swiftly, but she apparently knew nothing more. Corcoran had talked himself with the Fly, so she did not know where he had gone. The woman rolled her head wearily on the back of the chaise.

"There was nothing else...."

At an apologetic voice in the doorway, Wentworth turned to see old Jenkyns, his butler, standing there, wrinkled face harassed beneath a crown of curly white hair.

"Begging your pardon, Master Dick," he said slowly. "A gentleman wants you on the phone. He wouldn't give his name, but it's the same one that called you twice before today."

Wentworth strode toward him. "Quickly, Jenkyns."

The old man plugged a portable phone into a baseboard. Wentworth clapped it to his ear.

"Richard Wentworth speaking."

A suave voice laughed into his ear. "That is to say, the Spider speaking! This is your master, the Fly."

Wentworth's eyelids drooped until the gray gleam of his gaze was a slit.

"Bolstering your courage with words, Fly?" he asked softly.

A cry tore from Rosetta Dulain as she learned whom Wentworth addressed. She thrust herself up and started toward Wentworth, but Ram Singh stepped into her path. She shrank from him, to huddle again on the chaise.

Over the wire, the Fly was still amused. "Not at all," he replied to the taunt. "You have not bothered me at all, Spider. You have reached the scenes of my little coups only after their successful completion. Our brush in the park was scarcely enough to start the blood circulating well…."

Wentworth, gripping the phone hard, feeling once more the bitter futility of anger, recognized the Fly spoke the truth. The Spider had not even inconvenienced him.

"Despite those facts," Wentworth clipped words into the transmitter, "I warn you not to attempt anything at the opera tonight, or you may find yourself… *bothered.*"

Silence answered him, the silence of humming wires. A faint smile touched his lips. He spoke slowly: "Another thing. If harm comes to Corcoran, I shall withdraw my promise to meet you with swords. When I see you again, I will crush you like any vile vermin!"

He stopped then and let the silence swell between them. For a full minute it continued until the humming of the wires became tremendous, until they became like the evil wing-buzzing of a great poisonous insect….

"I perceive I have been indiscreet," the Fly broke the silence. "Still, I shall go through with my plans. A word to you, Spider. Keep your hands off; keep the information you have gained strictly to yourself."

Wentworth laughed. "Frightened, Fly? I thought the Spider couldn't bother you?"

For an instant, the Fly did not answer. When he spoke again, anger edged his voice. "You will keep your meddling hands off my affairs," he ordered, "or Corcoran shall die!

"You may inform Rosetta that Ginnie's life has been forfeited by her telling you of the opera. I have decided, however, to spare her life—I have other uses for the charming Ginnie. Remember! Hands off—or Corcoran dies!"

"Don't dare…" Wentworth's sharp words were cut off by the click of disconnection. He stood staring straight ahead of him, the phone clenched in his hand. No use trying to trace that call, he knew; yet he must act quickly.

The Fly had admitted he planned atrocities at the opera, had warned him that if he acted, Corcoran's life would be forfeit. Yet if he did not act, heaven alone knew how many might die!

Corcoran was as close to Wentworth's friend Kirkpatrick as if he had been an only son. And Wentworth was responsible for his falling into the Fly's hands. The Spider's face grew grim. Before this, he had been ready to sacrifice friends and loved ones on the altar of service to humanity. Regardless of the cost, he could not turn aside now. He must push on in his battle with the Fly. He held out the phone stiffly to Jenkyns, but his eyes were on Nita and Rosetta Dulain.

"The Fly has Corcoran," he said slowly. "He threatens to kill him if I act. Rosetta, he says Ginnie's life is already forfeit." The woman jerked rigidly to her feet. "But he says he will spare her life for other purposes." He met her eyes directly. "Will you help now?"

The woman got out hoarse words: "If I could, I would. I have told all I know."

Wentworth studied her for a full minute and a small gleam crept into his eyes. "Very well," he said, "we'll leave it like that." He turned to Jenkyns. "Get Commissioner Kirkpatrick on the phone. Ram Singh, I shall need the Lancia tonight. I'm going to the opera."

Going to the opera.

With four words, Wentworth cast Corcoran's life and his own into the balance, had hurled defiance at the Fly!

CHAPTER 12
DEATH AT THE OPERA

THE METROPOLITAN OPERA HOUSE is an old brick building aloof from the tinsel and gabble that is Broadway. The gay dance of red and blue and white signboards begins where the Times Building raises its triangular height at Broadway and Seventh Avenue. The river of light flows uptown.

The Opera House stands two dark blocks downtown and has a brilliance of its own, a deep glowing fire as of precious stones, an elegance that shows the paste and glass of Broadway's jewels at their true worth. The Empire Theater stands just across it on Broadway, but it is often dark. It was dark this night when rich cars began their stately parade before the Opera House where the Fly would strike. Their sleek procession formed a suave background for the incredible display of furred luxury and shining silks. Men's high hats gleamed; their canes had golden heads. A mighty harvest for the Fly.

So Wentworth remarked somberly to Kirkpatrick as they descended from the Lancia before this dimmer marquee. The faces of the two men were set in grim mold and they walked with deliberate stride to Wentworth's box in the Diamond Horseshoe, the wealth-bedizened semicircle of loges where society holds brilliant levee.

All about them, the two saw the preparations of the police. Holland and Kirkpatrick had worked out with Wentworth a detailed defense. Their forces, scattered among the orchestra seats, through the boxes, sprinkled among the hanging balconies, were everywhere.

There, on the stage, a golden voice soared into the magnificent *"I Paggliaci."* In the box, Wentworth turned grave eyes to Kirkpatrick.

"I do not see how further precautions can be taken," he said slowly, "but I feel also that these will not suffice."

Kirkpatrick's face was drawn. His pointed mustache was as dapper as ever, his bearing jaunty, but there was torture in his gaze. Childless, he had fastened his whole affections on young Corcoran. His pain, his fears for the boy were like a knife in Wentworth's heart.

There had been no reproach from Kirkpatrick, as there had been no hesitation in his decision to call in police despite the Fly's ultimatum of death. It was Corcoran's life against many.

Nita Van Sloan

"Corcoran would not wish me to do otherwise," Kirkpatrick had said slowly when told the circumstances.

Wentworth knew he was right and the undoubted courage of the boy was another twist upon that knife of pain. So he had sworn to himself that when he had done his utmost to thwart

Ram Singh

the Fly this night, he would gamble his life for Corcoran's in a daring attempt to free him.

Before the last sobbing note had dropped the curtain on Paggliaci, the nerves of the two men in the box were drawn to wire-thin tautness. All over the house, they knew, police, too, must feel the strain of waiting and watching for the Fly's attack.

That slow tightening of tension was not lessened by the knowledge that the Fly had worsted the police in every contest, that they had been able to learn nothing about him. Wentworth's plan to follow known criminals had failed to lead them to the lair of the Fly. It had only convinced them of the criminal's cleverness. For every man followed had eluded his shadow. That in itself was proof that the Fly was building an enormous organization. Why else would the crooks be aware of their shadows? Where else would they gain the skill to rid themselves of trailers?

The intermission was reached without untoward event. Always

the tension mounted, the apprehension of men who wait for a zero hour they cannot foresee against an enemy whose skill they know, but whose attack cannot be fathomed. The police, some uniformed, others in evening clothes, prowled among the unsuspecting crowds swirling gaily in the promenade, watching, watching… and still nothing happened.

Gray cigarette smoke rose above the animated chatter of the throng. Wentworth and Kirkpatrick strolled tight-muscled among them, watching, too.

The dowager Mrs. Cartwright, Wentworth remarked, wore her famed necklace of blue diamonds. Four hundred thousand was the least estimate ever put on that gorgeous matched string. Mrs. F. Hampton-Beverly wore a tiara featuring a single huge ruby that glowed like a fabulous wine. The wife of the Consul General of France—but the chronicle was endless, the wealth incalculable. This was, indeed, a harvest for the Fly….

WENTWORTH CURSED, lips drawn. A woman's voice went shrill and he whirled. Her shriek had been only laughter. Silly, this tension. But he could not rid himself of it.

He watched closely fifteen or twenty men circling singly through the close ranks. These were the police on watch. He spotted MacTivish. Joseph Stull strolled past. Still nothing happened.

Presently the crowds filed back to hear the exquisite *Cavaliera Rusticana*. Its matchless intermezzo was flowing beneath the leader's baton when the Fly struck.

Wentworth saw it first, a red, flickering glow from the highest balcony. He sprang to his feet, and from above, a shuddering scream of awful terror rang through the house. It crashed discordantly into the rising beauty of the intermezzo. The scream cried, *"Fire!"* Kirkpatrick leaped to Wentworth's heels.

"Get to the stage," Wentworth told him quickly. "If there's a panic, we don't stand a chance. Get to the stage! Hold the audience!"

Kirkpatrick whirled and ran long-legged for the stage. Wentworth streaked across the rear of the boxes where the wealthy were seated. That single shriek of fire was tossed back from the walls, repeated from every corner. Hell cut loose in the gallery. The red glow mounted. Women screamed and the hoarse shouts of men echoed through the vaulted hall. The bedlam of terror drowned out the frantic playing of the orchestra.

Fire! *Fire! FIRE!!*

The cry swelled from the boxes, from the orchestra. Jerking startled eyes back, Wentworth saw flames licking up the scenery. The side wall of the theatre showed a tracery of yellow fire running like water up its full height.

"Keep your seats, everybody!" Wentworth shouted. "Take it easy. It's all right! It's all right."

The flames were a mockery to his words. Kirkpatrick was a gesticulating, shouting figure in the midst of the stage. As he stood there, the asbestos safety curtain thundered down behind him, shutting off the dance of the flames there.

But only for an instant! The entire curtain collapsed, crumpled into an ineffectual heap of stiff cloth upon the stage. The blaze leaped higher and panic danced in mad fury among the audience. Stunned and horror-struck, Wentworth stood motionless as he realized the enormity of the Fly's plot. The fiend had even cut the guy-ropes supporting the heavy safety curtain! There was nothing to hold those hungry flames in check. Their hot breath puffed out into the faces of the frenzied crowd.

The collapse of the asbestos safety curtain snapped the final thread of reason. As if blown upward, the entire audience leaped to its feet with a concerted scream. Hoarse and shrill, inarticulate and senseless as the howl of a mad dog, the shrieks of terror soared to the vault, crashed back thunderously into the ears of those who shouted. It increased their madness.

Like wild things fleeing the grass fires of the plain, they plunged into the aisles, racing in frantic, pell-mell flight. There was one difference. Wild things had vast distances into which to flee. Here the hordes were hemmed in by walls. The first streaming wash of the panic hit an exit and surged backward. More men and women plunged against it. *The door did not open!*

Here in the Horseshoe, men and women moved with more restraint. Faces were white as the heat of those furious flames, eyes wide with horrid fright, but they held themselves in check. Wentworth raced ahead of their retreat and hurled himself against the bar across an exit door. He could not move it. He stepped back and lunged against it with his entire weight. It bounced back with only a slight shudder. Three times he assaulted and three times failed.

Had the Fly plugged all the exits? Had he denied these hundreds even that chance for life? Wentworth wrestled with the door. It was vain. He dashed to another. It, too, was jammed tight. The haze of the smoke was billowing down from the ceiling now, crowding down upon the heads of the frantic hundreds who fought desperately to smash the exits. Lights were dim yellow ghosts and the lurid glare of the flames were everywhere. The air had grown intolerably hot, a torture to breathe.

Wentworth's breath was panting in his throat from his futile battle with the doors. The bite of the smoke ate into his lungs and he coughed rackingly. He whirled and raced for a hallway, smashed a glass panel and wrested a fire axe from its rack. Back he darted toward the exit door, whirled the gleaming blade above his head, and struck savagely at the lock. The axe broke!

He caught the head and saw why. The Fly again! The handle had been sawed through, held together by a shred that snapped at the first blow.

THE TOUCH of panic brushed Wentworth's mind. For an instant he beat with futile fists upon the barrier of the locked doors. Slowly then, he fought himself to calmness. He whirled, realizing that none of the Horseshoe fugitives was crowding upon him. Dimly, through the haze, he made out the opposite wall and saw a door open there. The last of the occupants of the boxes was filing out.

A shriek over his head jerked Wentworth's eyes toward the gallery. A girl was poised on the railing. Even as he spotted her, the girl threw up her arms and jumped. A scream tore from her throat. Desperately, Wentworth sprang to catch her, scrambling over the backs of two rows of seats. He seized her as she shot past, felt the tearing rip of her weight against his shoulder muscles as they spilled to the floor together. Then the lights went out.

Wentworth fought to his feet, lifted the girl, and by the lurid flicker of the flames examined her. Her neck lolled laxly. His groping fingers found the vertebrae had been snapped. Wearily, Wentworth straightened. The smoke tore at his lungs now, shook him with coughing. The girl was dead. No use to wait here!

Distantly, through the bedlam of crackling flames, the din of screams and cries, came the spaced crack of pistol shots. Police were fighting the panic crowds, slowing the stampede. Wentworth staggered to the rail of the box. Through the smother of strangling smoke he made out the stage. Kirkpatrick had left that futile post. The entire platform, from back wall to proscenium arch, was a mass of red and yellow fire. The heat reached out and seared Wentworth where he crouched. He leaned weakly over the rail.

The police, he saw, were gradually getting the crowds under control. Pistol shots had cowed some of the rushes.

A few men had been wounded, dropped in their tracks as they fought for release. Battering axes rang now on the outside of the locked doors and Wentworth realized that firemen had reached the scene. Those who had survived the panic rush would be saved soon—but the Fly had won.

Yes, the Fly had accomplished his purpose despite all the precautions of police. The red specter of fire, the necessity of saving the stampeding audience hurling itself against locked doors, had made it impossible to watch for criminals. And meantime….

With a half-smothered cry of anger, Wentworth recalled suddenly that the door had miraculously opened for the occupants of the Horseshoe, the wealthy, jewel-bedecked women who sat in the boxes. He sprinted across the broad semicircle, sprang out through that one exit upon the spidery fire escape.

Below him, in a narrow areaway, was a huddle of people. The doors to the street were shut. He could make out the gleam of women's shoulders, of men's white shirts. Over them the lurid glare of the fire poured out through an open door. Men and women, every person in that packed areaway, lay prostrate upon the earth!

Wentworth leaped to the iron stairs, then hesitated. What had felled these people, laid them row on row like corpses in a morgue? Had they been shot… but that would have required inconceivably rapid work unless machine guns had been used. And he had not heard that staccato death laughter tonight. The only shots had been the deliberate slow fire of police. Then it must be—*gas!*

That tight, enclosed areaway would be like an execution cell. Poisonous gases were uniformly heavier than air. They would settle down upon that packed crowd like a fog of death. The Fly's men, with gas masks, could strip the bodies. Wentworth reeled back against the wall as he realized the enormity of the crime that had been committed here this night!

Even as Wentworth had feared, the Fly had been too clever for the combined forces of the police. He had not scrupled to imperil hundreds so that he might loot a few. The man was a fiend!

But had he already fled with his loot? Wentworth whirled back into the inferno of the opera house. Exit doors had been battered down. Everywhere the crowds were pouring out under the guns of police, the organized assistance of firemen. Streams of water were hissing on the flames.

Wentworth crouched and, holding a handkerchief tightly over mouth and nostrils, ran for the main entrance of the theatre. The Fly's main loot had been the jewels of the Diamond Horseshoe, but he would scarcely scorn the box office. As he darted into the hallway and rounded toward the manager's office, he abruptly halted. He squeezed his body tightly against the wall and peered intently ahead.

THROUGH THE smoke, he made out five bodies crumpled on the floor. He slipped to the nearest, crouched beside him. The man wore a police shield and he had been shot through the head. Wentworth cursed shortly. Surely, the Fly had been at work here! He caught up the policeman's gun, drew his own, and stole toward the office.

The door was closed. That might mean nothing, but why should escaping criminals, the loot in hand, bother to shut a door? The crackle of flames was close. Their hot breath filled the theatre, fanned by the draft of the many open doors. Wentworth smothered a cough in the crook of his elbow, crouched against the door. He heard a muffled blast within.

Wentworth's lips grinned back from his teeth. He flung open the door and went in with both guns spitting lead and death.

He had a blurred glimpse of four men huddled over a gaping safe, flashlights in hand.

Wentworth fired four times. Three bullets bored through the heads of the Fly's henchmen. The fourth smashed the arm of a man who stood behind the others, whose sharp voice uttered orders even as the Spider crashed in. As that fourth man staggered back, gripping his shattered arm, Wentworth sprang close and ground a muzzle into his body. He caught up a flashlight and sprayed its brilliance into the man's tortured face. It was not the Fly!

Wentworth cursed and raked the man's face with his gun barrel. "Where are you to meet the Fly?" he demanded.

The man's back struck a desk and he leaned against it weakly, staring at the lean, enraged face close to his own.

"Quickly," Wentworth snapped. "Talk, or I'll smash your leg and leave you here to burn!"

The man laughed jeeringly. "You can't scare me!" he swore.

Wentworth's lips parted in a thin, hard smile. He backed over to where the three lay dead upon the floor and stooped for a moment beside each, touching the base of his cigarette lighter to their foreheads. When he had finished, a hairy-legged crimson Spider gleamed on the brow of each—*the seal of the Spider!*

When Wentworth crossed back to confront the leader, the man's face was gray and his jaw trembled. He babbled pleas for mercy—and talked!

Wentworth slapped the man on the temple with his gun. He snatched up the bag of loot and, staggering under the double

101

burden of money and the unconscious crook, made his slow way out through the smoke to the street. A policeman raced to help him.

"More in there," gasped Wentworth. "Get them. I'll take care of this one."

He pushed on past two more police with the same excuse and found his car.

"Drive through the park," he ordered Ram Singh. "Head for Lexington Avenue and 147th Street."

When they were clear of the traffic jam, he pulled down the shades of the car and stripped his prisoner of his clothes, bound him hand and foot. Then he pressed a button beneath the left half of the cushion and the rear seat rolled forward, rotating as it moved. Its back was a neatly hung wardrobe. Out of it, Wentworth slid a tray of makeup such as actors use and folded upward a brilliantly lighted mirror.

Before this, Wentworth went to work on his face, glancing occasionally down at his prisoner. As he worked, he hummed snatches from the operas of the evening. The Spider was grimly happy. The Fly had triumphed this night, but at last the Spider knew his whereabouts and had a way to enter the stronghold.

There was a good chance, too, that he would be in time to save Corcoran. The fact that he was going, single-handed, into the headquarters of the cleverest, most ruthless criminal the world had ever known did not disturb him.

Wentworth's prisoner regained consciousness as they neared Lexington and 147th Street and stared upward blankly. His eyes widened with terror, for what he beheld was a man in his own clothing—and staring down at him with mocking eyes, was *his own face!*

WENTWORTH HAD little trouble getting all the information the man had. When finally he alighted from the car, he gave Ram Singh brief instructions to tie up the man in a nearby hotel and return to the address of the rendezvous.

The Hindu's dark eyes gazed with worship into Wentworth's face, but there was worry there, too. "Pardon, *sahib,*" he said in Hindustani, "but is thy servant to help?"

"Perhaps," Wentworth told him, "but first he should obey."

Ram Singh bowed even lower than usual, saluting with his cupped hands. "Forgive thy servant, master," he said, but still did not move to go. "I obey, but *sahib*… you enter the stronghold of this Fly alone?"

Wentworth frowned, hard lights in his eyes. "Since when has the Spider needed help in his battles?" he demanded sharply.

Ram Singh looked directly into his eyes. "The *sahib* is all-wise and all-powerful," he said, "yet this Fly hath a sting. He hath many men who kill and the spirits tell me it is not well… Take thy servant with thee."

For an instant anger stirred Wentworth; then he smiled slowly, for he saw that the Hindu was concerned only with the safety of his beloved master. And indeed the Fly was an enemy to be dreaded. Grim determination replaced the Spider's smile.

"It shall be as I have ordered it, Ram Singh," he said crisply. "*Sahib* Corcoran's life may depend on speed."

"*Han, sahib!*" the Hindu agreed and sprang to the car, drove swiftly away.

Wentworth watched him go, frowning. Rarely did Ram Singh oppose his orders; rarely did the faithful Hindu speak as tonight. Wentworth turned, rapidly moving toward 149th Street, but the frown did not leave his eyes.

It was not the first time that the Spider had gone single-handedly into the stronghold of the enemy. But never before had he met an enemy who triumphed at every turn; never had he met an enemy who played with the Spider—and escaped his fangs. For an instant he hesitated. Would it not be better to call police? Not for his own sake, but to make sure the Fly did not escape?

Looking down the dark narrowness of the street where the Fly held his rendezvous, Wentworth felt a cold finger of apprehension drag up his spine. Then he cursed. Damn Ram Singh for an old woman! If he called police, Corcoran would be dead when they entered. The Spider needed no help!

He strode briskly up to the doorway of the rendezvous and rang as his captive had told him. There was a smile on his lips—but in the back of his brain was still the small, cold voice of warning.

CHAPTER 13
FOREBODINGS FULFILLED

WENTWORTH STOOD on the step for a full minute, swiftly reviewing the routine the captured criminal had told him must be followed if he were to enter the Fly's stronghold, yet escape death in the traps that protected it. Suppose the crook had deliberately lied about one point of that routine so that he would be killed?

The Spider's shoulder lifted in a slight shrug. That act would sign the man's death warrant. Wentworth had made it clear that if he failed to return in a certain time, Ram Singh would wield his long-bladed knife slowly. Under those conditions, it seemed likely the man's instructions would be accurate.

But Wentworth could not delay. A small, mocking smile upon his lips—in the back of his brain still that cold, pointed warning—he put a forefinger on a small black button just to the right of the door. He pressed it twice, then counted ten slowly. No sound came from within, neither buzzer or bell. He pushed twice more, counted five, and pressed once again. Still no sound—but the door swung inward.

According to the criminal, the hall was a lethal chamber into which poisonous gases could swirl. Wentworth drew a deep breath and stepped in.

No one was visible in the darkness, half-dissipated by a vagrant light beam. As he cleared the threshold, the door swung noiselessly shut again and locked with a small clicking of the latch. Now all was impenetrable, almost tangible blackness. Two paces within the hall, Wentworth halted and began a slow count of twenty-five.

The black hall had the close, musty air of a place rarely opened. The heat was suffocating. A gas chamber into which poison gases would swirl if he failed to observe the formula of entrance to the letter! These conditions indicated that at least the man had not lied about a gas chamber in the hall. Wentworth held himself tautly. He coughed twice in the close heat from the smoke in his lungs.

As he finished his count of twenty-five, he took five paces straight forward. A silken curtain brushed his disguised face. A minute beam of light brushed his face and the air became fresh and cooler. Breath gusted from his lungs. He had left the gas chamber. The door had been operated by that beam of light which remained on for the barest fraction of a second, during which time he must pass the silk curtain and intercept it—or be asphyxiated.

One danger passed, but there were more. He halted again, counted twenty, and said in a deep voice:

"Lafayette, we are here."

Instantly a blaze of light showered down upon him. He was in the execution room. From behind panels of steel, through firing slits, men who knew every member of the congress of crime were studying his face and person now. If one detected a single suspicious thing, he would empty an automatic into Wentworth's body.

He stood unmoving, staring straight ahead. It was a full minute before his eyes became accustomed to the light and he made out a stairway to his right, a door at its foot, a hallway leading straight back. If he walked straight back that hall or started up the stairs, he would be shot down instantly, his captive had said. But suppose he had lied? Suppose he actually was intended to mount those stairs?

Wentworth calmly was counting seventy-five. At the end of that count he pivoted right and walked directly toward the door. The muscles between his shoulders were taut, in momentary expectancy of a bullet. He touched the knob and nothing happened. He opened the door and found a flight of stairs leading upward, twin to those outside. He went up the stairs slowly, carrying the bag of loot he had taken from his prisoner in the car.

With his left hand he removed his hat and drew his forearm across his forehead. "I get the jim-jams every time I come through that," he muttered to himself.

At the top of the steps was another door and he knocked on that in broken rhythm. The door opened and three men with guns confronted him. They said not a word, but removed his two guns. Wentworth walked in with a broad grin on his face.

"Boy, am I glad that's over!" he said.

Four men sat about a table spread with jewels. And the one at the end was the Fly.

THE FLY was smiling, lids half-lowered over black, intent eyes. His blond brows, the smooth yellow hair were meticulous. He wore evening dress, a white tie. The others of the group were less debonair. Their eyes glittered as they surveyed the heaped sparkling jewels before them. Mrs. Cartwright's necklace of matched blue diamonds had a place of honor. It occupied a bare spot in the middle of the table. Everywhere else the gems lay in little piles.

Wentworth opened his eyes very wide and stared at the table. He ran his tongue nervously over his upper lip.

107

Wentworth seized the Fly's legs and yanked....

"Geez!" he gulped. *"Geez!"*

"I am glad that you managed to escape, Gus," said the Fly pleasantly. "You were so long delayed that I began to fear for your health."

Wentworth pulled his eyes from the jewels with apparent difficulty. He looked at the Fly. The black eyes held his unwinkingly. They were brilliant, yet seemed opaque as a snake's.

"Huhn?" said Wentworth; then he gulped. "Geez, I'm sorry, but all that ice got me kind of cuckoo. What you say?"

The Fly pushed back a pile of jewels and their facets made light dance on the ceiling. He leaned his elbows on the table.

"Why are you late?" he asked slowly.

Wentworth frowned and heaved the bag up to the edge of the table.

"The cops hopped us," he said. "We got five of them; then another guy all alone showed. He was dressed like you. He came in and started shooting. I jumped behind the safe and let him have it. He backed out and I beat it. Then somebody chased me. I shook him and came here fast as I could."

"Are you sure"—the Fly leaned forward—"that you were not followed to the door?"

"Yeah," Wentworth said. "I pushed the guy trying to trail me under a subway train."

The Fly straightened slightly, face unsmiling, unwinking eyes intent. "And your companions?"

Wentworth shrugged. "Guess they got it in the manager's office. Least I ain't seen them since."

The Fly nodded slowly. He slipped his hand under his coat and leveled a revolver at Wentworth.

"Will you see, Butch," he spoke to one of the men without taking his eyes off Wentworth, "why Gus has a bullet hole and blood on his right coat sleeve and yet uses that arm freely?"

Wentworth looked blankly at his coat sleeve. He knew that he would find there just what the Fly said, but he was playing for time. Ram Singh had been right in his forebodings! Why in heaven's name, Wentworth asked himself, had he been so careful about other matters and forgotten that bullet he had put through Gus' arm? Another criminal might have missed the implication of that bloody sleeve, but not the Fly! To him, it was obvious that the man wearing the coat was not the man who had been clad in it earlier in the night. In other words, he knew because of that one fact that this was not Gus.

110

"I suspect, Butch," the Fly said softly, "that you will find the gentleman inside that coat is our estimable friend the Spider!"

Wentworth lifted a blank face. "Geez, Fly," he said, "don't be saying things like that. I took off my coat working on the safe and I reckon somebody shot a hole through it."

The Fly, gun fist resting on the table's edge, the barrel leveled competently at Wentworth's heart, permitted himself a slight smile.

"And your empty sleeve bled, is that it?" He started to shake his head, then didn't. "Really, Spider, I thought better of your inventive ability than that."

"Cripes!" Wentworth pleaded, watching the cautious circling approach of the man called Butch around the table. "Cripes, that blood must of come off one of the boys. I turned Fritz over to see if he was alive, and—"

Abruptly, Wentworth jabbed the satchel of money with his left hand, sent it skating down the table against the Fly's leveled gun.

ON THE instant, he dived beneath the table. Butch's gun bellowed. The Fly's legs straightened as he jerked to his feet. Wentworth seized the ankles and yanked. He kicked savagely at the shins of another man, then sprang up on hands and feet and humped against the table, spilling it crashing to the floor.

Shouts and curses, the crashing of three guns filled the tight little room with a madhouse of sound. Wentworth, lunging from beneath the toppling table, dived in a headlong tackle for Butch's legs, ducked his head beneath the flame lancing from the gun muzzle. The gangster smashed against the wall. His head thumped heavily and his body collapsed on top of Wentworth.

Wentworth got the gun, sprayed bullets ceilingward at the chandelier. The door opened and the three outer guards sprang in. Wentworth dropped one and the door crashed shut, leaving the room in complete darkness. Guns continued to blast. The Spider felt the body of the gangster on top of him jerk and quiver, heard lead plunk into it. He scrambled aside, dragged up the body, and heaved it toward the spilled table. It landed with a crash, and as it hit, Wentworth sprang soundlessly to the door.

He had had a twofold purpose in upsetting the table. For an instant it had blocked shots Also, it had spilled literally millions in jewels to the floor. In the darkness two of those men—there were four now—well might delay to pluck wealth from the floor while the Spider and the Fly fought it out alone.

Beside the door Wentworth stood tensely waiting. His captured gun was empty. Men cursed and scrambled on the floor. He gathered from the sound that at least one was belaboring the corpse of the gangster their own guns had slain. A tight, mocking smile touched his lips.

It had been comparatively easy to trick the gangsters. His quick move had even balked the Fly, secure for a moment in a tight room, four armed men to one without a weapon. But where was the Fly now? Wentworth thought swiftly. What would the Spider himself do? His most ingenious scheme would not be too brilliant to allot to the Fly. The man had shown himself the equal of the Spider in many ways.

But it required no great genius to figure this out. Obviously, in some manner, he would cover the door, expecting an attempt to escape. The smile on Wentworth's lips became twisted. Then the Spider would not attempt to escape!

Clutching the empty gun, Wentworth moved soundlessly toward where the scraping of feet, the grunting of struggling men showed where four still fought in the darkness.

CHAPTER 14
IN THE FLY'S TRAP

WENTWORTH ADVANCED inches at a time, feeling the way with a groping left hand and cautious feet. When the grunting of the fight seemed almost beneath his feet, he bent slowly forward. The extended fingers of his left hand touched hair and his right hand chopped in a short, savage arc. It crunched home and a man's breath hissed out. Another man cursed in surprise and Wentworth's gun slashed out again.

A scream split the darkness, a scream of pain that was half muffled. The steel of the revolver had clicked on teeth. Wentworth reached forward and struck twice more rapidly. The first blow missed; the second brought a dwindling groan as a second criminal sank unconscious.

With the second blow Wentworth dropped prone to the floor. Guns blazed through the blackness toward him. He fumbled over the bodies of the two men he had felled and found an automatic. Once more his lips smiled, belying the glint of battle hate in his eyes. He threw the empty revolver violently.

It crashed against the door. Two guns splashed flame at the sound and Wentworth's own gun crashed in tremendous echo.

"Three down," Wentworth counted.

He crept slowly forward, feeling his way along the overturned table, creeping toward where that fourth shot had split the darkness. But Wentworth was frowning now. There had been five gangsters in the room. Five gangsters and the Fly, after Butch had been killed.

He had accounted for four men and he was confident none of those had been the Fly. The Fly would not have been struggling on the floor with one of his own men, nor would he have fired at the noise of a thrown gun. That meant also that the fifth gun which Wentworth had partly spotted did not belong to the Fly.

It was possible that the Fly crouched in the dark, waiting until the Spider, grown overconfident in victory, should betray himself. But if that were true, why had not the Fly fired when the Spider had revealed his whereabouts by that last gun flash? The man had an uncanny accuracy with a gun. His slaughter in the bank attested that, for he had killed a half dozen with air-gun pellets, placing the lead so exactly that not one of those he had killed had cried out with his death wound. Yet the Fly had not fired!

That meant but one thing to Wentworth. Despite the fact that the room was without windows, despite the fact that the door had opened only to admit the charge of three gunmen, the Fly had escaped from the room!

His face grim at the thought, Wentworth continued his slow

advance. He was silent, but the one criminal who remained was not. He breathed with a slight rasp. It was difficult to place the sound. It might be two feet ahead on the right. It might be six feet ahead on the left. And that little difference might mean life or death to the advancing Spider.

He pushed on. Then he heard a sharp exhalation accompanied by a metallic click, a slight creak of a hinge. At the sound Wentworth clenched his fist tightly about his gun and leaped. For in those noises he guessed how the Fly had escaped from the room!

Plunging directly forward, he rammed against a man who cried out shrilly. Wentworth struck heavily with his gun, dived over the falling body and felt the wall swing silently away before his outthrust hand. It was, as he had guessed, a secret door! He caught himself, eased through the opening over a high sill, swung the door shut again. As he closed it, the base of his cigarette lighter touched for an instant. When lights came on, the Spider's seal would gleam there, claiming for his own the dead in the other room. There was a mocking smile on his lips. Yes, by all means he must leave his calling card. The Fly must not think him lacking in courtesy.

THE SEAL affixed, he stepped lightly aside and waited. Was he in another room where death would strike at him suddenly and overwhelmingly or was he in a secret passage? He was achingly aware that he had no idea how many shots were left in the automatic he clutched. He had no way of learning without putting the gun out of commission for a few moments' time, and that, too, might prove fatal.

He stretched out a hand to each side and found nothing. He crept slowly to his right. Four short strides in that direction he touched a wall. He turned along it, avoiding a chair that his groping hand located, and discovered a door.

He listened tensely beside it. A soft voice whispered outside: "… give the word," it said, "jerk open that door and cut loose with a machine gun. If the Spider hasn't already killed the boys, they'll have to take the rap. The Spider has broken the ring somewhere. Set? All right. Now!"

A machine gun stuttered in the hall. Wentworth yanked open the door and sprang outside. Two men stood there and one poured machine-gun lead into a darkened room. The other whirled. It was the Fly, and he held a revolver in his hand! Wentworth pulled the trigger as the Fly's gun came up. The Spider's hammer clicked on an empty chamber!

Wentworth hurled the gun straight at the Fly's face and plunged headlong in the same movement. He felt lead cut across his back, then his shoulder rammed into the man. The two slammed into the machine gunner and all three spilled to the floor in a savage, battling tangle.

As they struggled, a door jerked open, spilling white light into the hallway, and a half dozen men charged upon the fighters. Wentworth struck twice and knocked the machine gunner clear. The Fly clung to him with powerful arms. Wentworth fought desperately against them, but could not get free. The Fly's minions spread out warily, coming in with ready guns.

"Don't shoot! Don't shoot!" the Fly shouted. "Knock him out!"

Wentworth owed his life to the instantaneous obedience of the men. One of them had drawn a bead on Wentworth's head. At the Fly's order, he stepped in close to club his gun. Wentworth threw himself backward, pulling the Fly with him. As he pitched downward, he doubled his knees up against his belly and thrust them savagely against the chest of his enemy.

The Fly catapulted backward. He struck the first gunman and the two spilled heavily in the path of the others. Wentworth saw steps leading upward and, springing up, took them three at a time. It was dark above the stairs and the two bullets that sped after him dug harmlessly into the wood. He whirled the banister at the top, raced toward the rear. A window was there. Dim light filtered through it and outlined a small table in the hall.

Wentworth snatched up the table, hurled it crashing through the window and, snatching out the silken cord he always carried, made a loop which he dropped out the window. Instead of swarming down it, he raced wildly up another flight of stairs, making no sound that the pounding pursuit did not drown.

At the head of the steps, he crouched waiting. He heard a policeman's whistle going crazy out there in the night and wondered that no earlier alarm had gone out. Then he recalled that the first room he had entered had been without windows, guessed that it was soundproof. Only that savage chattering machine gun, the two final shots that had winged up the stairs in his wake, had been heard outside this tenement.

But police would be upon them in minutes now. The swift two-seated radio patrol cars, the four-seated detective cruisers would cut through the streets with shrieking sirens. Men would surround this place. The Fly must leave speedily, must desert this carefully designed headquarters. Wentworth felt an instant's fierce pleasure that this was so. He had struck one blow, then, at the criminals after so many defeats. Unless they were fast, they could not escape and much of their loot must be abandoned.

He watched three men cluster about the window he had smashed, saw them find the silken cord. For moments they searched the darkness below, then raced downward. Wentworth stole to the window, wrapped the cord about his arm under the coat sleeve and slipped silently down. He swarmed over a fence, ran through a tenement, and walked calmly out into the street beyond.

At the corner he found Ram Singh standing tensely beside the Lancia. As Wentworth strolled up, the Hindu whirled, hand flashing to his knife hilt. Then he smothered a cry of joy and sprang to the driver's seat. Wentworth climbed in behind.

"Go two blocks straight ahead," he said, "then circle at that distance. We must follow the Fly when he leaves."

He leaned back on the soft cushions, breathing deeply. How would the Fly escape? Underground passageways would not be impossible, but there had been no secret passages at the opera or in the Race National Bank. Yet the man had escaped.

Police autos were screeching past now. Off to the south, guns crashed out. A sedan spurted from a garage almost on top of Wentworth's car. Ram Singh braked to a sharp halt. The other driver wrenched violently at the wheel, rocked on the verge of capsizing, then darted down the street.

Wentworth dropped out in the shadows. "Follow that car, Ram Singh," he ordered swiftly. "I have other plans." He slipped off into the night and sped back toward where police battled the gunmen of the Fly!

CHAPTER 15
TRAIL OF THE FLY

HALFWAY DOWN the block, toward where police laid siege to the stronghold of the Fly, Wentworth ducked into a restaurant and bought a bottle of tomato catsup. Out in the night again, he tossed his coat over a fence and drenched his right sleeve with the red sauce. Then he watched from the shadows.

It was a half hour later that a policeman shouldered out of the Fly's fortress, herding a handcuffed man. While a crowd booed and catcalled, the cop thrust his prisoner into a doorway and stood guard with a drawn pistol. A slow smile touched Wentworth's lips. This was perfect!

Rapidly he circled to an alley end, entering the tenement from the rear, crept through a dark hallway toward the door where the policeman held his prisoner. In his left hand Wentworth gripped the catsup bottle, top off, contents thinned with water.

The prisoner stood dejectedly, leaning sagging shoulders against the wall. The policeman half faced him on braced feet, the gun dangling from his hand. Wentworth edged closer, drew the bottle back over his shoulder.

119

"Mike!" he called softly.

The cop whirled with a startled cry and Wentworth whipped the bottle forward spewing its contents squarely in the officer's face.

"Inside!" he barked at the prisoner and leaped on the cop. For an instant the crook stared wildly, then stumbled hastily into the darkness. Wentworth wrenched the cop's gun away, spun him about, and pushed him reeling into the street. The officer cursed wildly, swiping at his face with his hands. Other policemen converged on him at a dead run. Wentworth laughed and loped after the man he had freed. The catsup, thinned out as it was, couldn't hurt the policeman. It might sting his eyes a little, but they would be scarcely reddened tomorrow. The very unexpectedness of that mode of attack had prevented the officer from retaliating. Wentworth overtook the handcuffed prisoner as he groped out the tenement's back door.

"Thanks, Gus!" the man gasped. "Geez, I thought I was done for!"

He plunged out into the yard and ducked through an opening where a board had been knocked off a fence, then back to the alley that bisected the block.

"The tunnel! If we can make it, we'll be safe!" he panted back over his shoulder. He blundered into the wooden back wall of a private garage, lifted his hands fumbling above his head, and tugged open a door. Wentworth followed him inside and helped lift a trapdoor. They dropped through it and crouched in a shallow pit. Their breath was noisy in the narrow, dark hole. They listened tensely, neither speaking.

Heavy feet pounded up the alley. They hesitated, seemingly almost overhead. The pursuer cursed and the feet pounded on. The man laughed softly at Wentworth's side.

"Fooled 'em, Gus!" he whispered, exulting.

Wentworth heard him fumbling in the darkness; then white light sprayed from a torch in his hand. Wentworth slumped against the wall, and when the light touched his face, it was twisted in pain. His left hand gripped his right arm just above the elbow and the catsup made red streaks down his sleeve.

"Geez, Gus!" the man gulped. "I didn't know he plugged you."

"Didn't," Wentworth grunted. "Got shot at the opera tonight and a guy in a soup and fish took me prisoner. He gave me dope and made me talk a lot of stuff. Don't remember what it was. After a while I waked up and got loose. I got here just in time to see you marched out…" He broke off with a groan. "Look, we gotta get somewhere I can get this arm fixed up."

The man stood without a word, the bright light focused. Seconds slipped past without sound except their slowing breath. Wentworth straightened a little, ready for action. Had the man penetrated his disguise? Had he recognized that the stains were not blood? Wentworth's left hand shifted nearer the cop's captured gun.

FINALLY THE man spoke: "Guess we gotta get to the Fly," he muttered. "Only I don't know whether you ought or not."

"What the hell… you talking about?" Wentworth groaned.

The man explained the Spider's invasion of the Fly's stronghold disguised as Gus; how he had known all the tricks of entering the place. Wentworth cursed the Spider violently. "That's what that guy got out of me while I was doped!" he exclaimed. "The lay into the house." He cursed again and broke off only when the pain apparently made him faint.

"Look," he urged. "I gotta get to a doc or I'll croak. You take me to the Fly. He's a right guy. He won't hold it against me that I talked while I was doped."

At length the man agreed. "Okay, it's your funeral. I'll tell him how you sprung me. Maybe that'll help."

Wentworth pushed out from the wall, took two faltering steps, and slumped to one knee. He struggled to his feet again and the man threw an arm about his waist and supported him. This way the man would be handicapped if it came to a fight. They went like that through a hundred feet of tunnel, most of it a passage through two basements; then they came up in another garage where an old Ford was parked. The man cut the handcuff chain with a file and they got in the Ford and drove out into the street.

In the passing street lights Wentworth got the first glimpse of his companion's face. It was a dark, beard-smudged countenance and his right eyebrow drooped as if paralyzed. His hands on the steering wheel were tapered and sensitive. Slumped down in his corner with eyes nearly closed, Wentworth studied the man. The route he chose away from the police lines was clever; his movements, the alertness of his head's poise were vaguely familiar. A smile crept into Wentworth's eyes. Unless he was badly mistaken, this man was….

"Say," Wentworth drawled, pulling the gun awkwardly from his belt with his left hand. "Who the hell are you?"

The man jerked his head toward him and grinned. One side of his mouth remained stationary and Wentworth saw that the apparent paralysis of his brow extended to the entire half of his face.

"Speak up!" Wentworth snarled. "I never saw you around before. Hell, I saw the cop bring you out and… You knew the tunnel! Who are you?"

"It's quite all right, Gus," said the man gently. "It was necessary to assume a disguise so that the police would guard me carelessly and give me an opportunity to escape."

"Geez!" Wentworth gulped. "You ain't…."

"Exactly," the man said suavely with his lopsided grin. "I am the Fly!"

WENTWORTH ALLOWED his mouth to sag open in amazement, but inwardly he was laughing.

The Spider had rescued the Fly from the police! Rescued him because the Fly, alone and free from the toils of the police, could lead Wentworth to Corcoran and the girl. Apparently, in saving the Fly, he had put over the false identity as Gus, but he could not be sure. The Fly was clever in the extreme. All this seeming credulity might well be assumed to disarm him so that the Fly might learn the reason the Spider had sprung a criminal. He must proceed cautiously.

He gulped for words, praised the Fly's disguise, sputtered out again the story of being doped by the "guy in soup and fish."

"It's quite all right, Gus," the Fly said equably. "Your capture by the Spider cost me a number of men and a very valuable fortress, but in losing these I have gained an able and clever assistant. Tell me how you happened to devise that method of attack on the policeman."

Wentworth thought he detected irony behind the Fly's tones, but he could not be sure. He explained bumblingly.

"Geez, I dunno, Fly," he mumbled. "I couldn't use me right mitt and I didn't have no rod. I grabbed up a bottle out of a can to slug him with, then found out I couldn't get close enough to hit him. There wasn't nothing else to do."

"Excellent," murmured the Fly. "Nothing else to do. Oh, excellent, really!"

After three-quarters-of-an-hour slow drive, the Fly parked the car beside an apartment house in the West Eighties and led Wentworth carefully in by the tradesman's entrance.

They entered a large cellar room with low hanging lights. Suddenly, without warning, the Fly snatched the gun from Wentworth's belt. He sent him reeling with a blow on the back of the head. Wentworth stumbled forward. Instead of catching himself, he deliberately tripped and fell to the floor. He smothered a groan of pain, gripping his arm again, and rolled over feebly.

The Fly's disguised face leered down at him lopsidedly. "Did you really think, Spider," he mocked, "that I would believe a minion of mine could think up so clever a method of eliminating a policeman? No, no, Spider, your own smartness betrayed you. Then, too, catsup! And not very good catsup, either."

Wentworth stared up at him, then got to his feet, smiling

carelessly. "Geez, Fly," he said, imitating his earlier tones. "You're pretty damned smart, all right!"

The Fly smiled, but the poise of his body was alert; the black, direct gaze of his eyes beneath hazy eyelids was keen.

"I think," said the Fly softly, "that inasmuch as you defied my orders, it would be only fair if you were forced to witness the penalty inflicted upon Corcoran."

His tones were casual, but there was venom beneath them. Wentworth's smile stiffened on his lips. He studied the disguised face, seeking some similarity to the man he suspected of being the Fly. The cleverness of this disguise was proof, though, of an ability to hide identity completely.

"It is hardly necessary to inflict my penalty on Corcoran," Wentworth told him steadily, "since I am here in person to assume responsibility."

The Fly made no reply. He edged toward a dumbwaiter shaft and pressed the third button three times, kept the revolver trained on Wentworth.

"I could quote you many proverbs about that," Wentworth went on, smiling persuasively. "There is one in Hindustani." He rattled off words.

"So Ram Singh is here," said the Fly coldly. "Well, Ram Singh, if you move, I'll put a bullet through your master."

Wentworth laughed lightly. "That would do you no good, Fly, if the moment afterward a nine-inch knife slid through your heart. Ram Singh can throw unerringly up to fifty feet."

"Remember, Ram Singh," said the Fly, his voice growing harsh, "I fire at your first move."

Wentworth waved a hand carelessly. "It seems to be a deadlock, Fly. I see you have made a careful study of my technique and have learned my little habit of quoting Hindustani proverbs to Ram Singh. That makes it impossible for Ram Singh to do anything but kill you outright." He shrugged, smiled apologetically. "I would dislike to do that, but unless you immediately throw down your gun, I'll have to give the order."

THE FLY sprang toward the side wall of the cellar. Wentworth tensed for action, but the unwinking eyes held him unwaveringly. Abruptly the Fly jerked his head to the right to stare into the shadows behind him. Wentworth was twenty feet from him. The Fly figured rightly that even the Spider could not cover that distance before he could whirl and fire. But Wentworth was only five feet from the single light bulb that dangled on a loose cord from the ceiling.

Wentworth waved a hand carelessly, slapped it with a full swing of his arm and flung it to the floor even as the Fly whirled back with his gun leveled. The bulb slammed against a water pipe and exploded into darkness with a minute pop that was drowned in the crashing blast of the Fly's pistol. But he had fired at a moving target, and when darkness fell, the target had reversed its direction. Instead of darting off toward the dumbwaiter, Wentworth was sliding slow feet toward the opposite side of the basement.

Wentworth's smile was happy. The Fly still did not know that the order the Spider had shouted to Ram Singh would have gone unanswered. So far as Wentworth knew, Ram Singh was not within miles of this apartment house! He had turned the Fly's own cleverness against him.

But Wentworth must act quickly to take advantage of the situation. He knew now that Corcoran and Ginnie as well were prisoners in this building. If he could snatch them from the Fly's grasp and loose police on this second stronghold…. He doubted if that one shot, muffled in the basement, would bring them.

Masking his mouth with his hands so that the Fly could not locate him by his voice, Wentworth called out sharp orders in Hindustani. He altered his voice then and in curter syllables mimicked Ram Singh's reply. No shots sought him in the darkness and Wentworth stole softly forward again, creeping toward the dumbwaiter. Either the Fly had sought safety in flight or was waiting for help.

Reaching toward the dumbwaiter in the small service lift, Wentworth found the shelved box at the bottom. Using it as a ladder he climbed carefully to its top. Then, bracing himself across the narrow shaft, back against one side, knees and hands against the other, he began to inch himself upward.

He had passed the second floor before excited voices below, the diffusion of light into the bottom of the shaft, told him that help had come for the Fly. He caught only the sounds, no words, and so could not tell the course of the search. If they thought to flash a light up this shaft….

Wentworth hastened his climb. His knees had worn through his trousers and his flesh was scraped by the rough bricks. He had to be careful not to touch the ropes lest they rattle below and warn the Fly's men.

At long last he reached the third-floor level and braced himself there, listening. All was silence in that apartment. Quietly he eased open the door and peered into a brightly lighted kitchen. It was empty. He climbed in. The adjoining living room also was vacant and he peered into the bedroom beyond. A man sat in a chair tilted against a closed door, and the man had a gun held across his lap. Wentworth forgot the stiffness of his knees. That would be Corcoran's guard!

Wentworth hurried across the living room to the outside door. He opened it noisily, closed it again; took quick, stumbling steps into the apartment. He let his right arm dangle, still stained with the red of the catsup, and reeled into the presence of the guard. The man leaped up with gun in hand.

"Gus!" he cried. "How in the hell…."

He dropped the gun on the table and ran to help. When the guard came quite close, Wentworth swung a savage uppercut and stretched him cold on the floor. He paused only long enough to make sure the man would remain unconscious for ten minutes or more; then he snatched the gun, darted to the closed door. The key was in the lock. It was the work of an instant to un-fasten it, to race inside.

The only furniture in the room was a bed. Corcoran was spread-eagled on it, one hand or foot tied to each of the four posts, and a wadded gag in his mouth. Wentworth darted to the kitchen for a knife, ran back, slashed the ropes. As he worked, he talked swiftly.

"I'm the Spider," he said. "The Fly with some of his men is in the basement. When I cut you loose, I want you to get hold of Kirkpatrick by phone and get him to rush police here."

HE GOT the gag loose and the boy made croaking noises, trying to talk. Wentworth went on with his instructions. "He's not to strike until I signal, either by a shot or a shrill double whistle," Wentworth said. "Don't worry about Ginnie. If she's in this building, I'll find her and turn her loose."

He got Corcoran to his feet, helped him, stumbling, across the apartment. The boy still could not talk. He resisted feebly against his expulsion, but Wentworth permitted no delay.

"Hurry," Wentworth insisted. "Everything depends on your getting out of here and calling police! Can you walk now?"

Corcoran nodded and Wentworth started him down the fire stairs within the building and ran back to the apartment. He bound the guard in Corcoran's place. To a casual glance, it would seem the boy himself was still there. Then Wentworth made a hurried search, but failed to find the girl Ginnie.

He did find what apparently was the Fly's private quarters. It was fitted out elaborately with makeup equipment and disguises. Wentworth stood staring down at the dressing table with its mirror framed in neon lights and suddenly he laughed quietly to himself. He bent over and picked up a concave bit of glass, like an optical lens, but more curved. He frowned at it for an instant, then set rapidly to work.

He stripped off his clothing and hurled it out a window. Deft fingers tore off the makeup of the gunman Gus and built in its place a new face that had blond suave brows and a mocking mouth, that had smooth blond hair, a face with heavy-lidded eyes. They should be black and unwinking, but if he kept them in shadow, who could tell that he was the Spider—disguised as the Fly!

CHAPTER 16
FLY-TRAP!

WENTWORTH HAD barely completed his extraordinary toilet when the opening of the outer door let in a gabble of voices. "I tell you I heard the signal," one man was insisting angrily. "Didn't we hear a shot while we was going down? Wasn't the light busted?"

Wentworth got to his feet and strolled to the fore with mockery in his veiled eyes. From what they said, they had found no one in the basement. That meant the Fly had fled from the double threat of the Spider and the supposedly knife-armed Ram Singh; it meant the Fly might walk in at any moment and expose Wentworth's imposture.

But Wentworth was ready for that threat. He had expected to have to meet the Fly face to face and convince the arch-criminal's men that the actual Fly was an impostor!

He walked into the living room. "What did you find, my children?" he asked calmly.

Four men had just entered and they stopped in their tracks, staring at the suave blond man who confronted them. Their astonishment gave way to grins. A young gangster with curly black hair bounced forward on blithe feet.

"*Good!*" he cried. "Geez, we're lucky you escaped from that other house!"

Wentworth's heavy-lidded eyes regarded him unblinkingly. His fixed smile did not waver.

"Son of a pig," he said dispassionately. "You deserted me!"

The young man halted, began to stammer.

"You left my prisoner unguarded!" Wentworth went on.

The man whirled toward the room where the armed guard had sat.

"*Santa Maria!* Is he gone?"

He streaked into the room. Wentworth waited tensely. If his trick were discovered, if they found that a man had freed Corcoran and tied the guard in his place…. The curly-haired one bounced back jubilantly.

"We left Pete on guard," he said. "Don't know where he is now, but the guy is still tied to the bed."

Wentworth waved a careless hand and sauntered to a deep-cushioned chair in a corner, sank into it. The other three men, standing pegged in the entrance until now, relaxed their stiff fear and began to move about with a show of nonchalance. Wentworth was aware that they watched him as if he were a sleeping cat and they were so many wary mice.

"See about the other prisoner," Wentworth ordered shortly. The same man went toward the door. "No, wait," Wentworth said. "I'll go along with you."

He followed to the door and insisted with a mocking wave of his hand that the curly-headed one go first.

"Jerry," the man called back. "Lock that door in there and sit against it. If you stir, I'll take it out of you."

A red-headed man grinned. "Okay, Tony." He slouched off to stand guard and Wentworth followed Tony into the hall. The man hung back, waiting for him, but once more he was waved on with mocking deference. "After you, Tony."

Sullenly now, and puzzled, Tony led the way upstairs and fitted a key into a fourth floor apartment door. Three men scrambled up from a table scattered with cards and chips and stood watching. The room stank with stale tobacco; gray smoke eddied as Wentworth nodded casually and crossed with Tony to a door which he opened with another key from his pocket.

Wentworth looked over his shoulder into the room. He met blue, terrified eyes. A slender blonde girl sprang to her feet and stood tensely beside a chair where she had been sitting. The windows behind her were covered with steel shutters inside and white light blazed down from a ceiling fixture. A fan buzzed in a corner. There was a bed in the room, but it was smooth. She had not even thrown herself down on it.

His eyes took these things in, then came back to the terror in the girl's gaze. "Are you quite comfortable, Miss Clark?" he asked pleasantly.

Tony stepped into the room and to one side, and Wentworth saw a grin in his soft black eyes.

THE GIRL was dressed in a dark silken dress that was high at the throat and had bloused short sleeves. It was utterly simple, but set off her slender figure to perfection. Her mouth was soft and tremulous as she came hesitantly forward.

"Please," she said, "why must you keep me like this? There is no one to ransom me." Her diction was perfect, but there was the faintest of French blurring of the R's.

Studying her with the expressionless, half-closed eyes of the Fly, Wentworth decided that Corcoran had shown excellent taste.

"You are mistaken, my dear," he told her softly. "There is someone to ransom you." He smiled. "Myself!"

He bowed suavely and the girl flinched back as he took three slow steps toward her. Could he give her some hint of encouragement while his back was toward Tony? He decided against it. She was young, inexperienced. She might well betray him by a startled word.

The girl mistook the purpose of his advance. So apparently did Tony, for when Wentworth swung suddenly about to leave, the Italian was smiling with knowing eyes.

His face froze at Wentworth's cold stare and he ducked outside the door.

"I'll be back—later," Wentworth called over his shoulder to the girl and stalked into the outer room. He heard Tony shut the door and lock it.

"Everything set for tomorrow, Chief?" one of the three guards asked.

Wentworth turned slowly to face him. His mind rapidly analyzed the question. The Fly was planning some new infamy for tomorrow! What could it be? Where would his ruthless murderers strike next? He must learn.

133

"Yes," Went-
worth said quietly.
"Everything is ready.
Do you know your part?"

The man ducked a towhead,
grinned widely. "Sure do," he said. "All
I got to do is see them elevators jam in
the Race National soon as the men get up."

Wentworth nodded carelessly. "Right. If each
one does his part without delay, there can be no failure."

Good lord in heaven! Was there no end to the Fly's
daring? Apparently the Fly was not satisfied with the loot of
his previous single-handed raid on the Race National Bank
and was going to rob it again!

Wentworth sprang at the Fly, jarring the gun
aside and struck savagely with his fist.

He glanced slowly at the others of the Fly's men in the room. Should he ask them to review their parts and thus learn more of the plans for the bank holdup? He decided swiftly against it. These others might not have part in tomorrow's operations. He might expose ignorance that would betray his false identity.

Wentworth turned toward the exit and the door flung sharply inward, and a man stepped in with a leveled gun.

"Your little comedy has gone far enough, Spider," he said. It was the Fly!

"LET HIM have it!" Wentworth snapped at the four men beside him.

They half-started forward, but the leveled gun and the dead black gaze of the Fly stopped them. They turned incredulous eyes from the genuine Fly to Wentworth, and no man of them could say which was the impostor. The two men, identical in appearance, stared at each other with heavy-lidded eyes.

Wentworth knew that he could not hope to continue his imposture. The most he could hope to accomplish would be to stall for a few moments until he could signal police. If he failed to escape, if the police failed to crush this infamous company of criminals, the Fly would strike again tomorrow with all his fearful might! Scores more would die; a bank would be shattered! Wentworth must escape!

"I suppose you are the Spider," Wentworth said calmly to the Fly. "Though it's a trifle difficult to identify you in my own clothes." He looked him over from head to foot. "I don't blame my men for being fooled. I would be in for a shock myself if I met you unexpectedly. Accept my compliments on the perfection of your disguise."

The Fly advanced calmly into the room and Wentworth saw then that he had Tony's companions with him, that he had also the guard Pete whom Wentworth had tied to the bed in Corcoran's place. This, then, was why the Fly had not bothered to counter the Spider's verbal attack. He was sure of himself with these others at his back.

"Seize him, Tony," the real Fly ordered calmly. *"He* is the Spider in disguise."

Wentworth stormed. "This is utter nonsense! Are you all fools!" He whirled toward the towheaded one. "If you need identification, didn't I just tell you what you were to do tomorrow?"

The towheaded one stared at him with wide eyes, jerked his head in a startled nod, and looked at the real Fly with doubt on his face.

"Are you all cowards?" Wentworth demanded. He walked slowly toward the Fly's leveled gun. "You are the Spider," said Wentworth, "and the Spider does not shoot down unarmed men who are not attacking him. What in the world made you think you could get away with so brazen a trick as this?"

He was within five feet of the Fly. The Fly smiled, admiration in his face. "You can't get away with it," he said quietly. "You don't even know the names of the men in this room. Go ahead, call them by name."

That did it! The Fly had struck upon a simple way of proving his identity and Wentworth could not possibly compete with him. He knew in that instant that he was beaten, unless—In that instant, he acted.

Wentworth sprang. He jarred the leveled gun aside and struck savagely with his fist. The Fly reeled backward. His head struck a corner of the wall and he slumped to the floor, out cold!

Wentworth smiled down at the unconscious man. He called the only three men he knew by name.

"You, Pete," he said calmly, "Jerry, Tony, tie this man up, and tie him tight!"

For a full minute the gangsters stared at him with their mouths wide open; then they looked at the man prostrate on the floor.

"Well," Wentworth asked sarcastically, "are you waiting for the resurrection?"

"Hop to it, boys," Tony barked.

He strode toward the unconscious Fly and tumbled him roughly over on his face. The two other men Wentworth had named helped and in seconds they had bound him.

"Shall we scrag him, Chief?" asked Tony.

He looked up with a cold smile. He had the point of one of the Fly's own gold-hilted knives against the Fly's carotid artery.

Wentworth stared down at the unconscious Fly, at the knife which at a word from him would snuff out that life. It was just. The man had killed scores for mere money, had cold-bloodedly slaughtered innocents in the street so that his looters might escape. He had saved the Spider's life, but that was a personal matter and the Spider could not let such a consideration sway him. The Spider was judge and executioner. Should he not order now that this man expiate his crimes?

He opened his lips to pronounce sentence. He could not. Even though he condemned himself for it to the end of his days, he could not murder this man in cold blood.

There were reasons, of course, for keeping him alive. Even without his guiding hand, the powerful congress of crime he had assembled, the leaders of the Underworld united by him, would continue their reign. And only through the Fly could they be traced.

WENTWORTH SHOOK his head sharply. "Of course not," he snapped. "He's a thousand times more valuable to us alive than dead. Man, he's the Spider!

"Now, listen, Tony. Get this straight. Where the Spider operates, the police are sure to be near at hand. I doubt that he would have come into this building so boldly if he had not planned for police to follow. We've got to get out fast.

"Tony, take the girl and go to the Hubert Hotel. Register her as your sister and get adjoining rooms. Guard her with your life. Get going."

Tony nodded and crossed to the girl's room, unlocked it, and hustled her toward the hall. She cast an appealing glance at Wentworth as she was urged forcibly past.

"Jerry," he said, "you stay with me and we'll handle the Spider. The rest of you scatter."

The man Pete turned at the door. "Meet at the usual place, Chief?"

Wentworth nodded.

"Ask him," came the Fly's calm voice from the floor, "where the usual place is?"

Wentworth jerked his eyes to the man. He had recovered from the knockout and his dead black eyes glittered venomously up at the Spider.

"Where is the usual place?" the Fly demanded.

Wentworth laughed. "Still trying to get information?" he jeered. "Well, it won't do you any good."

He was swiftly calculating the chances while he sparred for time. There were seven gangsters in the room, all armed, of course. Wentworth had the Fly's gun in his hand now, but he stood no chance at all against all these men.

"That won't work," the Fly was mocking him. "What good would any information do a man who's tied hand and foot? Listen, Tom, Bill, Frank. Make him tell you where the usual place is."

Wentworth smiled carelessly. The Fly was turning his own trick against him, calling the men by their names. The Fly was shrewd. He felt a flashing sorrow even in the midst of his peril—that this man had chosen the wrong path through life. What a companion this man would have made in the cause of justice! What the Spider and the Fly side by side could not have accomplished!

But he had no time to think of such things. He must fight his way out of this room, take the Fly with him a prisoner.

He had just one advantage. He had a gun in his hand. The weapons of the others were in their holsters. But he was not yet ready to force the issue. He must give Tony time to get the girl out of the building.

"If it were true," drawled Wentworth, "that I am not the Fly, why didn't I let Tony drive a knife into your throat while you were unconscious?" He waved his left hand toward the seven men facing him. "You all heard me tell Tony not to kill him?"

Two of the men nodded their heads slowly. The others stared at him with frowning brows. Their certainty was wavering.

"Listen," said the man called Pete. "Don't get me wrong—I'm not doubting you, you know." Wentworth's direct gaze was on him and it disconcerted the man. He stammered over what he was saying. Sweat started out on his brow, but he kept stubbornly at it. "Why don't you just say where the usual place is, and—"

Wentworth smiled gently, but his eyelids drooped even more. His face looked lazy—and ominous. Pete stammered to a halt.

"I do not choose," said Wentworth softly, "to be catechized by my men."

He took two slow steps toward Pete, holding him with his eye. It was two steps nearer the door also.

"Suppose you explain, Pete, why you were not at guard over young Corcoran," he said. His tone was kindly. He took two more strides. He was within leaping distance of the door. He would have to leave the Fly here, but if Corcoran had done as he had been told, if he had summoned the police, they could smash this entire group.

"Cripes!" said Pete. "I was guarding him. And Gus came in and smacked me down, tied me up to the bed...."

"Who found out you were tied to the bed?" Wentworth cut in swiftly.

Pete's eyes strayed to the prostrate Fly, smiling upward mockingly. "He did!"

"I thought so," Wentworth snapped. "He found you because *he was the man who put you there!* He used the disguise of Gus once before tonight. He used it again to free Corcoran!" Wentworth laughed softly.

"You still haven't told them where the 'usual place' is," said the Fly from the floor.

"It's not necessary," said Wentworth casually. He stepped to the door. "Bring him along, Jerry." He turned the knob.

"Stop!" Jerry cried. "You're not the Fly. That scar on your temple…."

WENTWORTH SPRANG outside and slammed the door shut. He fired two shots through the steel panel and raced for the elevator. It was not at the floor and he darted to the steps. As he ran, he whistled shrilly twice. If only the police would strike now!

He whirled down the stairs, taking them in huge striding leaps, steadying himself with a hand brushing the wall. He reached the third floor, darted on toward the second. No sound from below indicated police were entering. He whistled again twice, raised his gun and fired a bullet into the ceiling.

He whirled into the hall on the second floor and a man darted at him with a raised club. Wentworth ducked, gun flying up. He stayed the shot. *The man was Corcoran.*

Wentworth cursed. The young fool must have disobeyed

orders. Good Lord! Had he prevented also the escape of Tony and Ginnie? But they were nowhere in sight. Perhaps Tony had used some secret exit…. As Corcoran struck fiercely at him again, Wentworth knocked the club aside with his revolver, seized the boy's wrist and twisted.

"Fool!" he cursed. "I'm the Spider. Did you call police?"

"You're the Fly!" Corcoran raged. "Let me at you and I'll…."

There was no time for delay. Feet were pounding down the stairs behind him. The elevator was whining up the shaft. Within moments, those seven gangsters, and there might well be others in the building, would be upon him. He hurled Corcoran from him, darted down the stairs. A grim smile flicked across Wentworth's face. Sometimes you could lead men where you couldn't drive them. His guess was that Corcoran could be led too.

As he plunged down the last flight of steps to the first floor, he heard Corcoran's feet behind him. Straight out the front doors Wentworth raced. He shouted Hindustani words into the night. He had put Ram Singh on the trail of a car that had spun from the same garage that later he and the Fly had used for escape. There was a good chance that by this time the Hindu was on hand.

He heard a weird whistle wail in the night and he whirled to the right toward the sound. Once more hope thrilled through Wentworth. Good! Ram Singh had followed his trail! Once more Wentworth shouted in Hindustani and heard the whistle. It came from a dark areaway beside another apartment house. Into that areaway Wentworth dived with Corcoran not two yards behind him.

A shadow detached itself from the wall and Corcoran grunted and slumped to the pavement. Wentworth leaned against the wall and spat out swift instructions to Ram Singh. For the shadow had materialized into the faithful Hindu.

"*Sahib* Corcoran is not hurt," Ram Singh said softly. "I but touched the nerves in his throat."

"Good," said Wentworth. "You have my orders correctly?"

"*Han, sahib!*" Against the dim light of the street, his deep salaam was outlined in black. "I saw the girl and a man leave the apartment by the service entrance, but delayed for your orders."

"Fine," said Wentworth. He darted from the areaway and checked in mid-stride. He snatched off wig and blond brows, began to rip the putty of disguise from his face. For in the distance, through the cool air of the graying dawn, he heard the whine of sirens. His shots in the halls of the apartment house had accomplished what Corcoran had failed to do, had summoned police.

Wentworth stole down the street and into the shadow of a dark doorway, where he watched the apartment. If the Fly and his men left the place, he would follow. If they remained, the police would capture them—unless there were some secret exit of which he did not know.

Headlights flashed, and a low-swung roadster swayed around the corner and roared up to the doorway. Two policemen sprang from it with drawn guns glinting in their hands. Scarcely had they hit the sidewalk when another car whirled around the other end of the block and squealed to a halt nose to nose with the first roadster.

Two of the men darted for the trade entrance; the other two strode briskly into the front door. Two more cars, one a roadster, one a detective cruiser carrying four men, slewed to a halt before the building. Wentworth waited, but though he watched until the increasing daylight threatened to reveal his surveillance, the police brought no prisoners from the apartment. He knew the answer, of course.

Once more the Fly, with the skill that only the Spider could match, had slipped through the cordon. Should he have killed the man while he had him helpless? Wentworth slowly shook his head. No, he had done right. It would do no good to lop off the head of the criminal alliance unless also he could dissolve the union. And the Fly alone could lead him to the others.

WEARILY, WENTWORTH turned his footsteps homeward. The night had not been entirely fruitless. Twice he had routed the Fly from his strongholds. He had wrested two hostages from his grasp—by now Ram Singh, following his orders, would have seized and turned over to police the gangster Tony and taken the girl Ginnie Clark in charge, but these things were not enough.

The Fly was still at liberty with all his men. There was a chance that the knowledge of a part of their plans having been betrayed to the Spider would deter the Fly from striking at the Race National, but Wentworth doubted that. The police had had advance warning of what was to happen at the Metropolitan Opera House and scores had died; uncounted wealth had been stripped from the bodies of the wealthy.

In doing that, the Fly had shown an uncanny knowledge of the plans of police. For he and all his men had slipped through a powerful cordon without difficulty. That fact was suspicious. Wentworth's eyes narrowed. He turned into an all-night restaurant. A newspaper hawker had ink-wet papers spread upon the counter. Wentworth purchased several, skimming through their stories of the opera holdup, printed in screaming eighteen-point body type. The list of the dead was like a page torn from the social register. Fifty bodies had been piled in that packed areaway, and Wentworth had guessed right—gas had been used there. Scores more had died in stampede and fire.

There were long columns that told of the terror of the people. There had been riots in City Hall Park as late as one-thirty in the morning after the fearfulness of the crimes had been revealed —that and the futility of the police efforts to stop the depredations of the Fly. Mayor W.O. Purviss had been in his office throughout the night. His major move against the Fly had been to restore Stanley Kirkpatrick to power as Police Commissioner.

"I have wronged him," Purviss' statement on Kirkpatrick read, "and I ask him now to accept my apology and to help the city in this, her hour of greatest need."

Wentworth barked a short laugh at that. As if Kirkpatrick, even as was the Spider, was not always willing to sacrifice face and honor and self to the cause of service to humanity! He turned into a telephone booth and called Kirkpatrick, congrat-

ulating him briefly on being at the helm again. He told him of
the plan to loot again the Race National Bank.

Kirkpatrick's voice was grim. "That points added suspicion
toward Joe Stull," he said.

"I disagree," said Wentworth briefly. "It seems unlikely that
he would risk suspicion by striking twice there. Here's another
point. Did you realize how completely police plans were known
at the opera?"

Kirkpatrick's tones grew sharp. "What do you mean?"

"Just that," Wentworth said slowly. "In this case no one can
be immune to suspicion. MacTivish has black eyes. I could
build quite as strong a chain of circumstances against him as
against Stull."

Kirkpatrick answered that with silence, finally agreeing that
what Wentworth said was true and saying that he would check
on the theory. Wentworth laughed suddenly.

"Kirk," he said, "I forgot the news I should have told you
first. Corcoran is no longer in the power of the Fly. Ram Singh
is holding him in security until he...."

"Dick," Kirkpatrick broke in and his voice shook with
emotion. "I can never thank you enough for that. I—God
knows—"

"Don't thank me," said Wentworth gaily. "The Spider turned
him loose and I stumbled on him unconscious in an areaway
and took him in charge. I'll see you at the Race National Bank."

Wentworth hastened then to his home. Nita met him at the
door—he had asked her to remain and keep Rosetta Dulain
under her eye and Rosetta was beside her. She held out plead-

ing hands. She had aged ten years, her face graven by lines of worry, her red hair no longer sleek and lovely, but a carelessly knotted mop atop her head.

"Have you heard anything of my Ginnie?" she begged.

Wentworth looked at her with expressionless eyes. "Within a few hours," he told her, "I expect a phone call that should give information. She has not yet been harmed by the Fly."

Rosetta Dulain dropped upon her knees, her hands stretched up to Wentworth. "In God's name," she pleaded, "tell me what you know."

"But I have," said Wentworth. "Will you excuse me now, please?"

He led Nita to a small private room which he called his den. The walls were lined with low shelves of books and above them the marvelous mellow canvases of many masters were hung. He sank upon a couch and Nita sat beside him, glorious bronze curls upon his shoulder.

"Why are you so cruel to Rosetta?" she asked, but there was no reproof in her voice. She knew Wentworth too well for that.

Wentworth's face was deadly serious. He gazed straight ahead of him, arm about Nita's shoulders. "That woman," he said, "is the key to this whole tragic case. She withholds information that would settle the Fly once and for all. She is not faking her worry, but as long as the Fly is in a position to harm Ginnie, she will not help us. It is her uncertainty that is torturing her."

"Maybe," said Nita softly, "if you could assure her that the girl was safe...."

"Maybe," Wentworth agreed dryly, and a bleak smile twisted his mouth.

IT WAS four hours later that the phone was brought to Wentworth where he and Nita breakfasted in the small room of books. Wentworth listened for three minutes, said "Good" twice and then, "Carry on, Ram Singh." He handed the phone back to Jenkyns. "Will you ask Miss Dulain to come here, please?" he said.

Nita's quick blue eyes were on his face. "Is the girl safe?" she asked. Wentworth nodded but volunteered no more information and Nita was silent.

Rosetta Dulain came hurriedly into the room. "Ginnie?" she asked. The word was a prayer.

Wentworth said, "She is safe, in a hotel under the guard of my servant."

For a moment the woman stared at him as if the words meant nothing to her. She raised her hand slowly to her forehead and wavered backward a step. Wentworth was just in time to catch her as she crumpled in a dead faint. He laid her on the couch and Nita bathed her temples with a wet napkin.

After long minutes Rosetta opened her weary eyes. Instantly she thrust herself up from the couch on rigid arms. "Where is she?" she cried. "Where is she?"

"I'll tell you that," said Wentworth grimly, "when you decide to tell me all you know about the Fly."

Haunting fear crept back into the woman's eyes. The strength went out of her arms and she sagged back upon the couch. "There is nothing more to tell," she said faintly.

Wentworth's mouth was a straight line. "Yes? And so this is how you repay me?" he asked tightly.

"But I don't know—I don't know!" the woman moaned.

Wentworth sought to make her answer, but Nita, watching him quietly, thought that there was hopelessness in his tones from the first word. For five minutes he questioned the woman; then, with a little shrug, he gave up.

"This is what I expected," he said grimly. "I know you're lying, but here's your sister's address. Claverson Hotel, Room 1218."

With a cry the woman dragged herself up from the couch. She snatched Wentworth's hand and kissed it.

"Oh, you are good!" she cried.

"Sure," said Wentworth shortly, "and you're so grateful."

He let the woman go, and fifteen minutes later started himself for the Race National Bank. There were deep lines about the tight pressed lips. His eyes were sunken with fatigue. He kissed Nita gently.

"Before night," he told her, "the Fly will be dead, *or*—"

Nita's arms tightened about his neck; her blue eyes were suddenly frightened. "Please, Dick," she whispered. "Please, there must be no—'or.'"

CHAPTER 17
LOOTERS' HOLIDAY

WENTWORTH RODE a taxi downtown through a city that was half mad with terror. Fresh editions of the newspapers hit the street every hour. Every minor crime in the city was attributed to the workings of the Fly, and his successes had emboldened the Underworld, sent its members looting and killing like ravening beasts.

The columns of the *Press* Wentworth bought chronicled the crimes in double measure down the front page and demanded redress or a new city government. It reported growing riots and crazed terror of the Fly, who struck so shrewdly and with such utter disregard of human life, with such ruthless efficiency.

The wind that fanned Wentworth's face was like the hot breath of these terrified millions within the city. It was fetid with the odor of heated asphalt, overheated engines, and exhaust gas. The people were frantic, but so intense was the oppression of the sun that those who must be abroad despite the terror merely moped along the streets. Wentworth's cab driver operated his machine listlessly, did not even rush changing lights.

Wentworth paid him off two blocks from the Race National. The sun beat straight down with heat of mid-afternoon. He peered into the blazing sky. A blimp with an advertising sign kiting behind it was drifting lazily across the blue.

The two blocks to the bank building were interminable. Wentworth's shoe soles seemed to curl away from the baking walk. He glanced down a side street. A group of men lounged idly against the side of an ancient church, listening to another man who stood on a soapbox in one corner of which the stick of a small American flag had been thrust. Wentworth nodded. Those men were police. Unless he guessed wrong, there would be a machine gun under that box.

He lifted his eyes and saw another dirigible with a kite sign.

He frowned, glanced about and located the one he had first seen—two of them. Wentworth's eyes narrowed with a tension that was not entirely due to the glare of the sky. Deliberately he stepped down from the curb, wove his way through desultory traffic, and looked upward from the middle of the street. There were four dirigibles aloft.

Wentworth hurried back to the curb, stood staring at the soapbox speaker. He turned and looked down Broadway. A crew of men was laboriously tearing up paving blocks with pickaxes and drills. Plenty of police on the ground, but there wouldn't be any aloft where those dirigibles floated. What was it that towheaded gangster had said was his job at the Race National? *To jam the elevators after our men use them.* Wentworth smiled thinly. Rather obvious, when you put it that way, wasn't it?

He spun into a cigar store and squeezed into a phone booth, called Kirkpatrick, was relayed to the temporary downtown office the police commissioner had set up.

"It's just a hunch," he said, after explaining about the dirigibles, "but I suggest that we get army planes with machine guns to head this way. If any dirigible touches on the roof of any building, *shoot that one down!*"

Kirkpatrick said, "Thanks, Dick. If that's a hunch, I wish I could have a few of them. It sounds like dead certainty to me. Some of the boys are working on that man you and Ram Singh brought to us—Tony. So far we haven't been able to crack him."

Wentworth spun out of the booth and, heat forgotten, strode swiftly toward the Race National. It sounded like certainty to him, too, that the dirigibles were manned by criminals. But it would take at least ten minutes to assemble men for the army planes and to warm up the engines, load the machine guns. Ten? It would be fast work if it was done in twenty! Allow ten more for the planes to reach the city from Mitchell Field, and you had a half hour in which the robbers could operate unhampered. And a half hour would be plenty!

An elevator shot Wentworth to the top floor of the Race National Building. He went directly to the door leading to the roof stairs, jerked it open. A man in the uniform of an elevator operator was smoking a furtive cigarette. He grinned. Wentworth slammed a left to the man's jaw and dumped him in a crumpled heap on the steps. He searched him and found two .45 automatics. He straightened then with a lopsided grin on his lips. Odd equipment for an elevator operator!

Swiftly he stripped the uniform from the man, tied him up, and locked him gagged in a supply closet which his ready lock-pick unfastened. Wentworth rapidly donned the uniform and, pocketing the man's two guns and his own, went to the roof. One of the dirigibles was drifting close by. A glint of glass in the gondola betrayed a pair of binoculars trained on him. Wentworth waved an arm. The man in the gondola did the same, and the dirigible circled into the wind and moved deliberately toward the bank.

WENTWORTH GLANCED about him and spotted a rope reel bolted to the roof. On the drum was a huge hook. There was gearing and a handle so that one man could exert enormous force on it. There was no doubt for what that was

Guns spoke at the same instant and Wentworth pitched to roof, firing as he fell....

intended! Wentworth sprang to it and watched the dirigible, its propellers fanning the air, nose downward and into a gentle breeze.

He swung a swift glance around. The other three dirigibles were circling toward other buildings! Wentworth cursed savagely. Why hadn't he seen the significance of *four* dirigibles? The Fly was robbing four banks at once!

Should he desert this post, dash down and phone a warning to Kirkpatrick? No, he could not. His warning would only disrupt the defense of this one bank. It probably would come too late to help the others. And this dirigible, seeing him run, might flash an alarm to the others and defeat his plans. It would be more than twenty minutes still before the planes could arrive....

As the dirigible drifted toward him, not fifty feet above the roof, a man lowered a stout rope from the gondola, a rope ending in a lashed loop. Wentworth set the hook in position on top the reel, darted forward and seized the loop, made the connection and instantly spun the crank.

The pawl clattered on the teeth of the rope drum as the gears meshed with oil-smooth speed. The beat of the dirigible's motors lessened, and with the tautening of the rope it settled slowly toward the roof. A second line tumbled downward and a man descended hand over hand. He darted to Wentworth's side and without a word threw his weight upon the crank handle.

The dirigible settled by the head, its tail swinging slowly in the gentle breeze, its motors barely turning over. Only one man remained in the gondola, and as Wentworth glanced up, he, too, swung to the rope and came down. The blimp was no more than ten feet above the roof now.

As the man ran toward them, Wentworth watched him out the corner of his eye. If either of these two knew the man he had knocked out and replaced.... Abruptly he sprang clear of the crank handle and snaked a gun from the breast of his uniform tunic. He beat the other man's draw by a fraction and his bullet crashed through the crook's skull.

The man working at the crank stared with surprise and terror mingled on his face; then he jumped clear, pawing for his pocket.

Wentworth waited until the man had a hand on his own weapon; then he drilled him between the eyes.

The pound of running feet whirled him about. Guns spoke in the same instant and he pitched sideways to the roof, firing as he fell. Two men in gas masks dropped huge sacks they carried and attempted to duck back into the kiosk exit of the stairs. The Spider's bullet helped one go. Its six hundred foot-pound impact hurled him backward down the steps. A second shot nailed a bandit to the kiosk door.

Wentworth got slowly to one knee, waiting with gun ready, but no more men came out. He crossed swiftly to the first criminal and hauled him to the rope reel, then carried the second up the stairs and laid him there also. The loot of the bank he placed beside the kiosk; then slowly he cranked the dirigible nearer to the roof. It bucked the wind, bouncing upon landing buffers, springing up again. A propeller brushed the gravel. But the gondola was within five feet now, low enough.

One by one, Wentworth went to the four corpses, pressing

the base of his cigarette lighter to the forehead of each, removing gas masks from two faces. When he had done that, a small spot of rich vermilion glinted in the hot sun, a small seal with sinister hairy legs and fangs, *the seal of the Spider!*

Wentworth tossed the bodies into the gondola of the bucking dirigible and severed the mooring rope. The blimp soared with the grip of the breeze and the Spider waved a mocking adieu. He stared into the east and saw a close triangular pattern of dots lifting from the horizon, increasing rapidly in size. He looked off toward the other three dirigibles. One was rising slowly; the other two still were moored to the roofs. Once more the Spider waved a mocking hand, then he turned to the kiosk.

Slinging the gas masks over his shoulder, he dragged the bags of loot to the supply closet, locked them with the now-conscious but helpless gunman, and turned to the elevators. A glance told him that they were stalled, their pointers stationary at various floors. The towheaded gangster had performed his part of the robbery well.

The steps then. Swiftly Wentworth began the descent. He had saved the loot of the Race National, killed four criminals, and captured a fifth, but there was a frown on his forehead. What was the significance of those gas masks? With a shudder of horror that stopped him in mid-stride, he recalled that in other robberies the Fly had used phosgene gas!

If they had employed that in the bank, the slaughter would not be confined to the lobby, or even to the building. That drifting creation of hell was one of the most deadly gases known to men!

FOUR FLOORS above the street, Wentworth halted his swift descent and went to an office. The place was deserted. He walked through it to a window that overlooked Broadway; then, for a moment, he hesitated, eyes on the floor, scarcely daring to gaze on the street. For no sound rose from that usually crowded thoroughfare, no bleat of auto horns, no rattle of streetcar, no gabble of close-thronged workers.

And silence meant horror.

Wentworth raised his eyes and the color was swept from his face; his heart bounded violently into his throat. He reeled backward and collapsed into a chair. Death had walked Broadway!

Sidewalks were thick with motionless bodies. Automobiles had smashed through shop windows and others had crumpled nose to nose. Flames licked sickeningly over one such wreck. But nowhere in that street below was any sign of life. There was no motion.

Wentworth stared vacantly ahead of him. What difference did it make that the criminals who had perpetrated this horror were dead? That the loot they had sought was recovered? Hundreds, thousands had died that the Fly might snatch once more at millions!

Why, why had he not killed the Fly when he had lain helpless at his feet? But even as he asked himself that question, Wentworth knew that the death of the leader would not have averted this catastrophe. The plans had been already laid; each man knew his part. No, the robbery would have gone forward; these hundreds would have been killed even if the Fly had died.

With the Fly alive there was still a chance to snare the whole company of crime.

After long minutes Wentworth's stunned senses began to operate again. He heard the distant spluttering bursts of machine guns. For a moment he was startled. Could the dead of the streets come to life? Then he realized what it was and he laughed, laughed until his body trembled. It was not a pleasant sound. The planes were machine gunning the dirigibles of the Fly. Splendid! Let them burn here and in hell, too!

Wentworth realized that he was staring at a telephone. He snatched it and called Kirkpatrick, scarcely daring to hope....

"Thank God!" he gasped when the commissioner's precise voice clipped words into his ear. "Kirk, for God's sake, keep everyone out of the downtown area for hours. The street is full of gas and dead men...."

"I know." Kirkpatrick's voice was hoarse with rage. "Almost every one of my best men died down there and I'm marooned in this office. But they won't escape!"

"No," said Wentworth, "they won't escape. Some have already paid. The planes are firing on the dirigibles. But tell me where you are. I've got two gas masks I took off dead men. Before tonight, Kirk, the Fly will be dead, the Fly and all his vile congress of looters!"

CHAPTER 18
CONGRESS OF LOOTERS

DONNING ONE of the captured gas masks, Wentworth descended to the death-ridden first floor. Bodies were everywhere and he moved rapidly through the lobby of the bank, searched in offices and behind the cages, his eyes narrow behind the thick lenses.

The rounds completed, he waded through the ranks of corpses, thick-piled around the exit, out into the lifeless street. And here, too, with a sick pain at his heart, he scanned the dead faces. His mouth became a hard lipped gash of anger. The reckoning would come soon; soon.

He swept the skies with his glance. Only two dirigibles remained aloft and over one of those the yellow flames were licking. Darting army planes circled and loped, pouring more fiery bullets into the gray bags.

At last Wentworth reached the office where, five floors above the street, Kirkpatrick and a staff of men were marooned by the gas. Kirkpatrick rose wordlessly and stretched out a hand for the remaining gas mask. Wentworth removed his own.

"Before we leave," he said rapidly, "will you order a general alarm for the arrest of Joseph Stull?"

"On what charge?" Kirkpatrick spoke slowly. His face was distorted with care, the dapperness of his mustache gone.

"Murder," said Wentworth. "Arson, anything. Just get him in custody."

"You think he is the Fly?" Kirkpatrick asked, still slowly.

161

Wentworth shrugged. "You know the evidence against him, his swordsmanship, his absence from the bank during the first robbery, the fact that he had offices in the same building, that there was no possible way to escape from the building—and Stull turned up inside it. I have learned that he was good, too, in amateur theatricals which would be invaluable in disguise. He has no alibi for any of the Fly's operations." Wentworth drew a deep breath. "I just went over the bank thoroughly and he is not among the dead. I know of no reason why he should not have been at his desk to die with the rest."

Kirkpatrick nodded. "What about MacTivish?" he asked.

"MacTivish is dead," said Wentworth. "His body is in the lobby of the bank."

Kirkpatrick turned to an assistant and ordered the arrest of Joseph Stull. Holland bustled into the office, walking springily, a cheerful smile on his face.

"I've got a clue to the Fly," he said jubilantly. Wentworth and Kirkpatrick looked at him without words. Holland's blue eyes were as fresh and eager as a child's.

"Who is he?" Kirkpatrick asked steadily.

Holland shook his head. "Haven't got that far yet," he said. "But I just got this information by telephone." He raised a slip of paper, reading from it. "In the Hotel Claverson, Room 1217 this morning, a woman called the desk and asked someone to come quickly to her room. When they got there, they found a note thrust in the side of the mirror. It was addressed to the Spider and signed by the Fly. It said:

This time I have taken Ginnie permanently. Soon I shall have my other hostage again, too. He shall die. The girl—I have other uses for her.

Holland's grin wouldn't come off his face. "I know what girl that is. It's the little blonde who was with Rosetta Dulain in the Marlborough that night. I have a pretty good idea where she is, too, and through her I'll catch the Fly."

Wentworth nodded slowly. "Good luck," he said. "Our paths may cross." He handed a gas mask to Kirkpatrick. "Unfortunately we have only two masks."

Holland laughed. "I have one, too," he said. "I remembered that attack on the armored trucks and brought one along, just for luck."

"Why didn't you equip the men?" Kirkpatrick snapped angrily, then reached out a hand in apology. "Forgive me, Holland. Of course you couldn't. After all, it was just a hunch. Going with us?"

Holland shook his head, eyes merry. "No, I want to do this alone. I'm afraid more than one man might bungle it."

Wentworth nodded slowly. He could sympathize with that view. "Look out," he said somberly, "that the Spider doesn't get you."

He pulled the mask over his face, adjusted the straps and nosepiece, waited for Kirkpatrick, and the two strode down the steps and out of the building like two strange beings of another world. When they had reached the police lines and passed on into the safe zone, Wentworth entered a phone booth, called his home.

"Any word from Ram Singh, darling?" he asked Nita.

"North on Lenox," Nita replied. "Call me from the 145th Street Bridge."

KIRKPATRICK TOOK over a radio roadster and its siren parted the traffic for them. From the bridge Wentworth phoned again. "Go north on the Grand Concourse" was Nita's next message.

Wentworth explained rapidly while the roadster crossed the bridge and streaked northward. "Ram Singh is following a trail in successive taxis," he said. "As he changes from one cab to another, he has the driver call Nita and tell what course to follow. We can't be far behind."

"This is going to be ticklish work," said Kirkpatrick. He glanced at the white-fronted apartment houses sliding past them along the wide-parked boulevard with its three major lanes. "The Fly will have a hostage. I don't see how Ram Singh could have followed him from the hotel without being spotted."

"Ram Singh isn't following the Fly," said Wentworth briefly. "Stop at that next corner. There's a drugstore halfway down the block."

Nita gave him an address on the Grand Concourse. Wentworth raced back, a queer figure still in the purplish bank uniform. Kirkpatrick and the car were gone!

A taxi driver held up a finger and jerked his cab backward toward Wentworth. "Guy in the police car said tell you something about a hot trail," he said. "I didn't catch just what it was."

Wentworth sprang into the cab, gave an address a few numbers from that which Nita had relayed from Ram Singh.

He was frowning heavily. What could have pulled Kirkpatrick away when he knew Wentworth was close to the end of the chase? Only one explanation: he had seen something that looked even more certain, something on which he could not delay action. A quick smile touched Wentworth's lips, but left his eyes bleak. Well, they might meet—soon.

The cab cut from the wide central roadway into a side passage of the Concourse and slowed to the curb. Wentworth paid the driver off. "Sorry I didn't get all that message," the man said, "but the guy was off like a bat out of hell."

Wentworth nodded and walked slowly up the Concourse, whistling a weird, quavering tune. He passed the doorway of the address Ram Singh had given and was opposite the trade entrance of the next building when a low whistle sounded. He turned leisurely into the entrance, went down a flight of steps into the half-dark of a cellar passage. A man lurked in the shadows, a man in a turban.

"On the eighth floor of the next building, *sahib,*" the man whispered. "There is a way over the roofs."

"Good, Ram Singh," said Wentworth. "Have you your knife?"

"*Sahib,* I have two!"

Wentworth grinned in the darkness and followed Ram Singh through the damp, grateful coolness of the cellar to the foot of a shaft to which the automatic elevator descended at the touch of a button.

From the top floor, stairs led to the roof and a ladder Ram Singh drew from concealment spanned the fifteen-foot gap to the next roof. They reached the one beyond by the same process, and drew the ladder after them.

"This is the building, *sahib*," Ram Singh barely breathed the words. "They number not above twenty."

Wentworth nodded and drew the two captured automatics. He had reloaded one with shells borrowed from the police and he had his own lighter weapon.

"Twenty-one shots, Ram Singh," he said quietly.

"I have my two knives," said the Hindu, and his eyes were bright.

Wentworth's own eyes were smiling. He moved into the lead now, opened carefully the kiosk door that led to downward stairs and slipped from the brilliant light of noon into the comparative gloom of the upper hall. Ram Singh was at his heels. As they stood there, staring downward, the criminal Wentworth knew as Jerry opened a door into the hall below. He stepped out and looked suspiciously about.

"Ram Singh," Wentworth whispered. The Hindu slid past him and the man below jerked his glance toward them. His mouth opened and his hand whipped to a gun. Ram Singh's arm flashed down. Steel glinted in the gloom of the hall, gleamed through a narrow shaft of sunlight, and Jerry hunched against the wall, hands plucking at the knife hilt that protruded from his throat. He took two staggering steps and fell.

"Get his key," Wentworth ordered and passed the body without a glance. He pressed an ear to the door, heard confused voices within that were dwindling slowly. Steel touched Wentworth's hand.

"Here is another gun, *sahib*," said Ram Singh.

WENTWORTH SHOOK his head. "There are a number of men just inside the door," he said softly, "but from the sound I judge they are filing into another room. Keep the gun. When I open this door, you go directly to the passage between the two rooms and hold it."

"Han, sahib!" The Hindu's voice was eager, and once more the smile touched Wentworth's lips. In a battle like this he would rather have Ram Singh at his back than any other man. He took the key which had been removed from the dead criminal's body and slipped it silently into the lock. They would be expecting Jerry to return. He donned the Spider's mask, turned the knob carelessly, and stepped into the room.

His first swift glance told him that at last he had run to earth the congress of looters! There were faces here he knew, the faces of the leading crooks of the underworld: Limey the Pete, one of the best safecrackers in the world; Penman Charlie, an incomparable forger. Charlie was snarling with surprise and terror, fumbling for his gun. Wentworth drilled him through the heart.

Five men were in the room, one of them dead now, and Ram Singh already had sprung to the door that opened on its far side. As he went past Limey the Pete, the long-bladed knife in his left hand slashed out and Limey reeled back with a bubbling scream. The bubbling was caused by the blood in his slit windpipe.

But the other three men in the room were in action now. After the first stunning surprise their hands had flown to their guns. Wentworth leaped toward the nearest man, automatic in his right hand blasting. The other two criminals, throwing swift lead, found their companion's body between them and the Spider. That body took their first shot.

There was no time for a second, for Wentworth's two weapons spoke together and one crime congressman took leaden death through a blue hole in his forehead, the other raised on his toes with surprise and life gasping together from his open mouth. His heart had been torn apart by a crashing .45 caliber bullet.

Ram Singh's gun had been talking in the doorway and now Wentworth sprang to his side. Four men were down in there and Ram Singh's knife slashed into the throat of the fifth as the Spider's gun began again to mete out his stern justice. Seven men still were on their feet in this room, seven men who crouched behind flimsy chairs, behind a long table that must have been intended for the meetings of this congress of crime.

Two more men fell before Wentworth's deadly fire; then Ram Singh dropped to his knee with a bullet in his thigh. He fired the last two shots of his captured automatic into the body of the man who had wounded him. Only four left now: two behind a davenport, one prone on the floor behind the bodies of two of his companions, a fourth close against the wall behind the door.

Wentworth took him first, firing through the door; then he dived into the room, rolling. Three bullets dug into the floor about him. His swift change of position revealed one of those behind the davenport and his bullet spattered the man's brain over his companion in hiding.

The crook behind the rampart of bodies reared for a shot—

and Wentworth's two guns were empty. He hurled one violently at the man's face. Instinctively he ducked and Wentworth sprang for him. The gun seemed to explode in his ear, but his hands were upon the man's throat. He jerked him to his feet, whirling to use his enemy as a shield.

His eyes jerked toward the final gunman and he realized he had miscalculated. He was exposed to the man's fire and it was too late to interpose the fighting hulk of the man he held by the throat, The killer's automatic was leveled, his eyes were gloating…. Steel whispered past Wentworth's back. The man's eyes grew startled; a cry gushed from his mouth and he tried to jerk his body aside. The gun exploded wildly, then dropped from nerveless fingers. The man stood stiffly against the wall, hands rising. Ram Singh's knife had pierced his throat and crunched into the wall behind him. He died that way, his body sagging on the knife. The blade sliced slowly upward with the pull of his weight.

Wentworth exerted his full strength into the strangling fingers he had clamped upon his immediate enemy's throat and felt the man die beneath them. He dropped the body like a rag and at the same time the corpse of the man Ram Singh had knifed pulled clear of the blade and slumped with a soft thump to the floor.

A slow frown narrowed Wentworth's eyes behind the slits of his mask as he looked over the dead. He had wiped out the congress of crime in ten bloody minutes, but the Fly was not among them.

Until the Fly died, there could be no safety for the nation.

169

That man alone could rally the cohorts of the Underworld and launch them again in looting massacres!

Where was the Fly?

CHAPTER 19
TO THE DEATH!

WENTWORTH WHIRLED to Ram Singh. The Hindu already was binding his wounded thigh. He smiled wholeheartedly with a flash of white teeth. *"Wah!"* he grinned. "It is as nothing, *sahib!* Are there no more to kill?"

Swift admiration lighted the Spider's eyes. He well knew Ram Singh's bravery, but the fresh evidences of it never ceased to delight him.

"No more for you, brave one," said Wentworth softly, speaking in the Hindustani he knew Ram Singh loved. "Stand guard here." He tossed his cigarette lighter to the Hindu. "Yours the honor, Ram Singh. You yourself shall imprint the seal of the Spider!"

Ram Singh caught the lighter deftly, dragged himself to his feet, and drew proudly erect. Wentworth crossed the room of his vengeance toward a door in its far wall. If the Fly were in this apartment, it must be in that room beyond.

His own gun in hand now, Wentworth jerked open the door… and stopped in his tracks, staring in amazement.

Behind a rich desk of glossy walnut, a man slumped dead in a chair, the gold hilt of the Fly's knife protruding from his chest. There was a paper before him half covered with neatly penned words. Slowly Wentworth walked toward him, peered down at the note. It read:

> You are the better man, Spider. This is the end.
>
> THE FLY.

The dead man in the chair was Joseph Stull! Wentworth stared at the dead man and shook his head slowly, eyes slitted behind his mask. Abruptly he turned away and crossed to the window. The wall was sheer above and below. There were no fire escapes. Autos were slewing to the curb, men pouring from them, police in blue uniforms. On the walk stood Stanley Kirkpatrick, gesturing orders.

Once more Wentworth glanced swiftly about the room. A closet door was just behind the dead Stull, and as he looked at it, Wentworth heard a dull thumping within. He crossed to it in a bound, yanked it open. Above a handkerchief gag the blue eyes of Jack Holland greeted him.

Slowly Wentworth nodded. He turned to the desk and snatched up the suicide note of Joseph Stull, wadded and thrust it into his pocket; then he turned back to Holland. Behind him was a slender leather case that was familiar. Wentworth opened it and revealed the handles of two sabres.

He whisked out a blade and slashed Holland's ropes and gag with a skillful point.

Holland scrambled to his feet, grinning ruefully.

"My clue brought me here all right," he said, "but they were too many for me. They took me prisoner."

Wentworth laughed drily. "Excuse me, Mr. Holland. It is

clever, but it won't work. You could not have followed the clue of Ginnie Clark to this place because, since I took her from you last night, *Ginnie Clark has never been out of my hands!* Would you be kind enough, Mr. Holland, to accompany me to the roof?"

Holland shrugged, eyes intent on Wentworth's mask. "If you insist, I can't very well help myself, can I?" he asked.

"Not very well," said Wentworth softly. His sabre point was at Holland's throat. He shifted its position to the loin above the kidney as Holland walked slowly past him. As they entered the outer room, Ram Singh was imprinting the last of the Spider seals upon the foreheads of the dead. He straightened, dark eyes switching from Holland to his master.

"Ram Singh," said Wentworth softly, "we go to the roof. Will you see that we are not disturbed?"

The Hindu salaamed. *"Han, sahib!"*

On the roof, Wentworth faced Holland, the two sabres bare across his forearm.

"I swore," said Wentworth, "that we would meet again with sabres to the death." He whipped off his mask and revealed his grim smile.

Holland touched his tongue to his lips. "I don't know what you mean," he faltered. "I remember no such promise."

"I mean," said Wentworth softly, "that you are the Fly!"

"My dear fellow," protested Holland. "You saw that it was Stull! You yourself pointed to the case against him."

"I did that for two reasons," said Wentworth shortly. "One that I still was not sure whether the Fly was yourself or Mayor

Purviss, the other that I knew Stull was in deadly peril and you wanted him saved, if possible, from being killed and left to take the blame for all these crimes.

"BUT, I know you are the Fly, Holland. I'll tell you why. That note left in Ginnie Clark's room undid you; the note that was addressed to the Spider and signed by the Fly. You knew you didn't write it and suspected I planned some trap, but you didn't know what that trap was. So, in Kirkpatrick's office, you read the note aloud to give you an excuse to be on the premises of this stronghold of the Fly's in case you should be caught.

"You thought you would turn my own trick against me, but you didn't, Fly, you didn't."

Holland shook his head slowly. "Pardon me if I seem obtuse, but what has that note got to do with your ridiculous charges?"

Wentworth's smile showed grim amusement. "Just this, Fly. You held Rosetta Dulain to the course of action you outlined by making her think you would harm her sister Ginnie Clark. It was nice psychology. See what you think of this:

"I told Rosetta I had saved Ginnie from you, which was true. I tried to make Rosetta talk, but she was still afraid. She would not tell me where your hideout was located. So I worked a little trick on Rosetta. I sent her to the room where Ginnie had been hidden, and when she got there, Ginnie was gone and she found a note addressed to the Spider and signed by the Fly..." Wentworth broke off, for Holland's face had tightened, its ruddiness paled.

"Ah, I see that you understand, Holland. When Rosetta saw that note, she became convinced that you were no longer threatening to harm her sister, but that you actually were harming her! She had kept her side of the bargain to betray me, but you had played her false. She was furiously angry. She set out for your hiding place to make you pay for your betrayal.

"Simple, eh, Fly? Ram Singh, my servant who placed the note in Ginnie Clark's room, simply followed Rosetta to your hiding place, then phoned me where you were. I don't know where Rosetta is now, but your guards evidently frightened her off and I imagine she's lurking about somewhere now waiting to blow holes in your trimly athletic body."

Holland shook his head emphatically. "What I said was true," he insisted. "I came here, following the clue of Ginnie Clark."

"But, my dear fellow—" Wentworth began, then shrugged. "I don't see how you can maintain that position. Ginnie Clark has never been near this place. Perhaps it was her astral self you followed?" His smile grew mocking. "There are other counts against you, Fly. You have been present on every occasion when the Fly made his mysterious disappearances.

"You could easily accomplish that, being one of the police. You, as the Fly, simply got out of sight for a few minutes, stripped off the disguise of the Fly, and showed yourself in your true identity—Jack Holland, Deputy Commissioner of Police. That not only enabled the Fly to disappear, but it made young Jack Holland seem very clever. He was always on the scene of the crime ahead of, or simultaneously with, the first police to arrive.

"Also, Holland, I have learned that though you are an excellent *sabreur;* you have concealed that fact very carefully. The Fly has few equals with the sabre."

Holland was frowning now. "I still do not see that any of this proof is conclusive," he said slowly. "Nor is the fact that many of the police plans were known to the Fly any stronger evidence against me. And there is one fact you overlooked, a fact that would free me in any court on earth.

"A half dozen persons have sworn the Fly had black eyes. Mine are blue!"

Wentworth laughed, and presented the sabres across his arm again. "That, Holland," he said softly, "is what convicts you. When I used your makeup box in that Eighty-sixth Street apartment and assumed your identity, *I discovered your trick!*"

Holland's eyes narrowed, his lips set. Here, at last, was the mask of the man who had dueled the Spider. "What do you mean?" he asked quietly.

WENTWORTH SCOOPED a small concave piece of glass, thin and slightly smaller than a spectacles lens, from his pocket. He tossed it to the gravel roof where it tinkled into fragments.

"That was your trick, Holland," said Wentworth. "It is German optical glass.* The invisible type that is used by actors and other

---

* AUTHOR'S NOTE: An interview given to a New York newspaper recently by a well-known optician described a new eyeglass lens, invisible because it was curved to match the curvature of the eyeball and fitted beneath the eyelids, directly against the surface of the eye! Sounds painful? It is, at first, the story goes on to explain, but the lenses are worn only brief periods at first, being dipped before fitting into a saline solution. Before many days, the eyeball becomes accustomed to the lens and moves freely within

persons who must depend on appearance, yet must wear glasses. The glass fits beneath the eyelid directly against the eyeball. You must wear it sparingly at first until you become accustomed to the slight pressure, but it does not take long."

"I still don't see how that would turn my eyes black," Holland jeered, but his fists were knotted at his sides.

Wentworth smiled. "You simply painted a black iris on that lens, leaving a small hole in its center for vision. That was why you never winked. That was why you had such a fixed, intent regard. And that is why, when you looked to one side, you always turned your entire head lest your blue irises slide out from beneath that black spot and be detected."

"You are clever, Mr. Spider," sneered Holland, "but you were a fool to come to the roof alone with me. For I shall kill you now and claim double credit for the Fly below and for the Spider up here. Your evidence shall die with you!"

As he finished, he snatched the hilt of one of the sabres and danced back on guard. Wentworth lifted his sword, eyes glinting behind its shimmer in the bright sun.

"Don't be a fool, Holland," he said. "You will notice we stood quite near the door to the stairs. Kirkpatrick has heard every word."

it—and invisible spectacles are an achievement. They are used chiefly by actors and other persons whose appearance is extremely important, yet who must wear glasses at all times. The glasses are expensive, costing from $75 to $90 a pair.

"Then he knows you are the Spider!" Holland jibed as he came in swift as light with a feint and wicked thrust.

Wentworth laughed. "He knows that you called me by that name! That is all!"

Then the laughter faded from his lips and he began a slashing fierce attack. He drove Holland back, pace by pace, toward the rampart at the edge of the roof. There the Fly staged a rally. His sabre flickered with the speed of light. With a singing slash of steel he wrenched Wentworth's blade from his hand and sent it spinning across the roof.

Wentworth darted after it. Holland took a swift pace in pursuit, then whirled toward the rampart. He snatched up the ladder Wentworth and Ram Singh had used and with it he spanned the fifteen-foot gap to the next building. He was mounting to it when Wentworth snatched his sabre from the roof. He was halfway across before the Spider could reach the rampart.

"Hold!" Wentworth cried fiercely, "or I'll run you through from behind!"

Holland turned on his precarious perch as Wentworth sprang to the ladder. Their swords clashed. Below them yawned dizzy space. Their feet rested on the slender rounds of the ladder between staves not two feet apart. But their eyes were not for these things, not for the police shouting in the streets below, men who moved like midgets. Their eyes were solely for each other, for the swift thrust and parry, the feint and ringing steel.

Once Wentworth's point flicked through and snagged the flesh of Holland's throat, but it no more than pierced the outer skin. Once the Fly's edge brushed Wentworth's forearm and drew a fine thread of blood. Holland's face grew desperate. He began a furious attack, so fiery that Wentworth was forced to retreat a precarious round. But his sword was a rampart of steel before him through which the Fly could not penetrate.

He battered at it so that the day sang with the ring of their swords, the singing music of tempered steel. Suddenly Holland lunged, sliding a foot forward along the edge of the ladder. And as he lunged straight at Wentworth's throat, he dropped forward until he lay almost prone along the ladder, body supported by his left hand braced against a round.

His lunge grated on the Spider's sword, for instantly Wentworth thrust. And it was Wentworth's blade that went home. The upturned edge slashed past the Fly's face, slicing his cheek. The point slid home above the collar bone. For a moment the two were as motionless as statues, a frightened, pained expression on Holland's face. Then his hand slipped off the edge of the ladder, and he toppled into space. And Wentworth stood alone on that slender bridge, watching a dead man tumble like a limp-armed dummy into the void beneath.

HE GLANCED up just before the body hit and looked into the blue eyes of a woman. She stood panting against the far rampart, staring down gloatingly into the depths. Her fiery hair was whipped by the wind and in her right hand she grasped a knife.

Wentworth smiled faintly. If the Fly had vanquished the Spider, he still would not have escaped. There was always a vengeance for those whose crimes are too great.

"Rosetta," Wentworth called to the woman. She jerked her head up, staring.

"Rosetta, you did not play fairly with me. I had to trick you to find the Fly. But, Rosetta, I am playing fair with you. Ginnie is safe, still in my hands. I will take you to her if you will tell police that you saw us enter—just in time to catch Holland escaping. I have need to arrange an alibi."

The woman nodded. "I should make amends to you for the wrong I have done."

Together they walked to the kiosk door and Wentworth bowed gaily to Kirkpatrick. "The Fly is dead. I took that honor from the Spider, but—" he shrugged—"the Spider was before me with the others. To him must go the credit for wiping out the Prince of the Looters and his congress of crime."

Kirkpatrick smiled slowly. "I saw the work of the Spider," he said. "I congratulate him—and you, Dick." He held out his hand. "Sorry to have left you that way in the street, but I saw Holland pass in a car with Joe Stull. I followed them here, then went for help."

It was an hour later that Wentworth stepped back from the door of his apartment and allowed Rosetta to enter first. She darted in on quick feet, then stopped, staring at a girl with silvery hair close in the arms of a boy who smiled across her shoulder.

"Hello, sister," the boy called gaily to Rosetta. It was Corcoran!

The girl—it was Ginnie Clark—pulled from his arms and ran to Rosetta, threw her arms about the woman's neck. "Oh,

Rosetta, we were married this morning, Corcoran and I. Mr. Wentworth sent that Hindu servant of his and got me away from that criminal and then the Hindu sent Corcoran and me away and told us to stay in the hotel, but—but—"

Wentworth was smiling, his weariness forgotten. Nita stole up to him and linked her arms through his, smiling too. She turned her deep blue eyes up to his, but there was still a shadow over their brightness.

"Is it—is it all over, Dick?" she asked hesitantly.

Wentworth stopped smiling and nodded.

"It is over," he said slowly. "The Fly is dead!"

A little cry fluttered from Nita's throat. She flung her arms about Wentworth's neck and buried her face against his chest. Slowly his arms went about her. Another of those little moments stolen from death and peril and pain, a moment when Nita and Dick need think only of themselves.

But this time, Corcoran, seeing them, did not tiptoe away with a sad smile. He laughed and taking Ginnie's hand, he extended his other, palm downward, over Wentworth's and Nita's bowed heads. He made his voice as deep as a cardinal's and intoned sententiously:

"Bless you, my children!"